REBECCA'S

Unlikely matches of the t

by K A Fleming

Copyright © 2024 by K A Fleming

All rights reserved. This book or any portion thereof may not be reproduced or used in any manner whatsoever without the express written permission of the publisher except for the use of brief quotations in a book review.

Printed in Scotland.

ISBN 9798301875953

First Printing, 2024

Publisher: Leather and Silk Publishing, Edinburgh

CHAPTER ONE

The new Duke of Sandison had not long returned to the Ducal estate to fulfil his role after being summoned home due to the sudden decline of his father's health, leading to his death, not thirteen months previously. Alexander Fane always knew he would one day take on the historic title, but at just eight and twenty he had hoped he would have been an older man when the responsibility fell on his shoulders.

The heir to the Sandison estate had been travelling Europe enjoying the finer things in life; savouring the most exquisite wines and eating in the elite dining rooms of Paris and beyond. Alexander made good use of his English heritage and lineage which impressed many; this was also helped by his striking looks, allowing the Duke access to the finest establishments around. He also left many a broken heart in his path as he travelled various countries without a thought for what or who he left behind, able to relax and do as he pleased without the scandal sheets and the prying eyes of the ton watching his every move.

Now Alexander was home, it felt like an age since he had stood in his father's study which was now his domain. It felt much smaller than he remembered, drab and unremarkable. As a young boy, he would sometimes join his beloved papa, quietly amusing himself in the corner playing with his precious toy horses and hand-carved soldiers, content to be close to his adoring father. The late Duke enjoyed his son's company just as much and would occasionally screw up pieces of parchment into little balls, throwing them at Alexander as he played, much to the young boy's amusement. Looking out of the large rain-soaked window, the duke smiled as he recalled his idyllic childhood, often a rarity within the families of the aristocracy. He rested his palm against the coolness of the glass, his shirt sleeves rolled past his forearms, revealing tanned skin and a slight covering of dark hair, his father's signet ring adorning his pinky finger.

The weather had not relented since his return, the large well-kept gardens becoming waterlogged, the rain battering the footpath, leaving puddles almost pond-like. He had not witnessed weather like this for some time, although there were days during his travels when he longed for the refreshing feel of rain on his warm skin. Looking down at the ring he wore, fidgeting with it, twisting it and gently rubbing his thumb over the initials embellishing the heirloom, he thought of his father and how he missed him.

Releasing a shaky breath, Alexander settled behind the large mahogany desk littered with correspondence relating to his many business interests and family estate matters. As Alexander had had no dealings with the estate for several years, taking for granted that his father would live much longer than he tragically did, he had much to familiarise himself with. Being educated from an early age in the ways of business and estate management meant that he was not completely naïve about his duties.

He was also thankful that he had an estate manager who had worked for the family for many years, a man dedicated to his father, reminding himself that he must get to know the staff; he had barely spoken to a soul since his return other than his valet, leaving things as they were in the capable hands of his mother. Sifting through ledgers, Alexander did not know if he was imagining what he thought to be the faint smell of his father's pipe smoke, even though months had passed since his death.

'I must get the curtains laundered to rid the room of the smell.' Speaking aloud, he was conflicted about whether the familiar smell was also of some comfort to him.

He had loved his father dearly which was uncommon in his set, many sons hating or being estranged from the ruthless and heartless men they called father. Hence, why he had promised the previous Duke throughout his life that he would make him proud when he one day took over the Dukedom, his father not doubting this for a single second.

Lowering his head, Alexander closed his eyes, clasping his hands while resting his elbows on the desk, an unruly lock of jet-black hair falling forward over his forehead. But his silent contemplations were immediately interrupted. The sound of feminine laughter brought him back to matters at hand: his sister, Emma must be taking afternoon tea. He frowned, already aggravated by the unladylike noises coming from the drawing room.

Growling to himself, Alexander got up and made his way across the room to shut the door, hoping to drown out the incessant giggling. Reaching out to grasp the handle of the heavy oak door, he was greeted by the sight of his younger sister practically skipping along the hallway towards him, her pale yellow dress floating gently behind her, a book clasped in her hand.

Emma had grown into a vision of loveliness, but he knew that beneath that angel-like exterior, she had a rebellious streak, a wicked sense of humour, and a vocabulary that could best any gentleman who dared to cross her, especially when it came to the rights of her sex.

Not long past her twentieth birthday, with hair as dark as his own, perfectly styled in the latest fashion, the apples of her cheeks were slightly pink from what was no doubt unsuitable conversation between unmarried ladies.

Standing with her hands behind her back, it was obvious to Alexander that the book she was trying to hide from him was not entirely suitable for the young and impressionable, such as his sister. Not having the time or inclination to question her, he continued to pull the door closed.

'Brother, Brother,' Emma called out, trying to catch his eye when he tried to avoid her, 'Shall you come say hello to some of my dearest friends? They have yet to be introduced to you since your return. They are quite keen to meet with you, although I have no idea why.' She smiled.

His heart sank to the floor; the idea of making polite conversation with giggling debutantes, fluttering their pretty eyelashes behind elaborate fans while imagining themselves as his new Duchess, filled him with dread. Being away for so long had meant he was out of practice in dealing with young ladies of the ton. During his travels, he had satisfied his lust with more experienced women, mainly wealthy widows enjoying newfound freedoms after being repressed by controlling husbands. He knew that there would be a time when he must marry a suitable lady, a lady that would easily fulfil the role of Duchess. The mother to his heir. Knowing that his own parents had truly adored each other, a real love match was uncommon but not unheard of. Alexander knew that his marriage would unlikely be one of true love. He had high standards when it came to his family name now that he was the Duke and believed his future wife should be a lady who had been primed to become a Duchess from birth.

'I am rather busy with estate business, my dear Emma. Another time?' His answer was curter than he had meant it to be, but he really was not in the mood.

'Oh brother, you are such a bore! You have barely left this stuffy old room since your return; the pallor of your skin is no longer full of colour as it once was. It is decidedly grey. You used to be quite handsome,' his sister gibed.

'*Used* to be? I will excuse your impudence on this occasion, sister, but if it continues, you will have no more visits to the modiste for two seasons.'

Responding to Emma's comment with a slight smirk to the corner of his mouth, he knew that it was unlikely that she would still be on the marriage mart for two more seasons. The season was well underway, and he imagined that his home would soon be a hive of activity from the delivery of extravagant floral displays to visits from would-be suitors. The thought made his head ache.

Emma acted as if she had not heard him, giving the sly expression that he had seen many times since she was a young child contemplating mischief, culminating in some prank or other, so he braced himself.

'Sister, you have that look...' Before even finishing his sentence, Alexander found himself being grabbed forcefully by the wrist and pulled in the direction of the drawing room, the chat becoming louder and the laughter increasing as they got closer.

'Ladies, ladies, let me introduce you to my elusive brother, his grace the Duke of Sandison,' Emma declared almost theatrically.

After the announcement, the room descended into silence, the only sound being the gentle rustle of silk skirts and the placing down of teacups. The duke was trying to conceal the annoyance he felt, thinking of a suitable punishment for his sister for this awkward predicament she had put him in.

Three pretty women sat upright waiting for introductions. These were not young girls who fluttered their eyelashes or swooned behind oversized fans, these were ladies who looked at him with a confidence and self-assurance that was unfamiliar to the ton. Of course, they wouldn't be marriage-hungry debutantes; these were Emma's friends.

Alexander was just about to take a quick bow before excusing himself, keen to return to the peace of his study, when hurried footsteps came rushing down the hall, undoing the awkward silence. The sound was accompanied by another voice unknown to him. His back was currently turned, facing the ladies in the room, when he heard yet another female approaching. Groaning to himself, he shook his hand free from Emma's grasp, ready to retreat.

'Lady Emma, it is as you said. The library on the first floor is quite magnificent, it would be perfect for the ...'

When Lady Rebecca Rutherford caught sight of the tall, black-haired gentleman just inside the doorway with his back to her, she took a breath and a slight stumble, her ungloved hand reaching to cover her own heart as she let out a gasp. He stood with one hand casually resting on his hip, drawing attention to muscular arms, arms that were bare to the elbow. Rebecca willed him to turn so she could see his face.

'Rebecca, there you are. I must introduce you to my dearest and most favourite brother, the Duke of Sandison, your grace, Lady Rebecca Rutherfo ...'

Before Emma finished her introduction, Alexander turned. He was more handsome than she had hoped, the look of disdain on his countenance further intriguing Rebecca. Her days were filled with reading dark and gloomy novels, and she thought this gentleman would be a perfect character in one of the tales. Her imagination running away with her, she pictured him living a reclusive life in a Gothic mansion, petrifying anyone who dared come near.

'I am your only brother, Emma', he spoke through gritted teeth, his deep masculine voice sending a shiver through Rebecca, her eyes drawn to his full lips as he spoke.

Rebecca looked at Emma and then at her brother, unable to prevent herself from letting out a stifled giggle which came out more of a snort; this prompted further sniggering from inside the room, which quickly shut down when Alexander turned his head and gave one of his icy stares. It was not the comment, but his serious expression when doing so that incited the giggle to escape Rebecca's lips. She had never been concerned about how she was portrayed in society and would never bow down to anyone, whether they were a Duke or not.

Glaring at Rebecca, reeling with what was either anger or mortification, Alexander wondered who this insolent creature was that stood before him, this friend of his sister.

Did she just laugh at me? Does she not know how to behave in the presence of a Duke?

Alexander scornfully looked to his sister who had now joined the other three ladies of the group. She was seated on one of the rich velvet sofas, carefully watching the duke's reaction to her friend's unladylike actions. Emma could not be bothered with his snobbish attitude since gaining his new title, so took great joy in his displeasure.

I must speak to mother about the company Emma keeps; she needs to learn how to behave now she is the sister of a Duke.

Rebecca remained at the duke's side, waiting for him to move so she could pass and rejoin her friends in the drawing room. The surly gentleman still stood in the doorway, his large physique towering over her, a faint scent of what smelt like lavender emanating from him. Alexander had noticed her pale green eyes as soon as he had first seen her. They were now bright with curiosity, dipping discreetly to admire his bare arms, unconsciously biting her bottom lip which could easily have caused his trousers to tighten; thankfully he was not some young lad with no control over such things.

Still rattled with the young lady that he now knew was named Rebecca, Alexander couldn't bring himself to take his eyes off her. Staring at her for longer than was acceptable of an innocent young lady, he had not failed to notice her bare hand as it rested on her beating chest moments before. He also had not failed to notice her rich chestnut hair that was piled loosely on top of her head and the way the thick wavy tendrils hung loose, grazing the flawless skin of her face. Her cheeks flushed slightly when she looked up and saw him looking directly at her, her rosebud lips slightly open as if she was about to be chastised for doing something she shouldn't. She was the most beautiful creature he had ever seen. Although she had a look of innocence, her eyes and lips told a different story; he could see the passion in them as she looked him up and down. The duke felt a masculine sense of pride as her eyes roamed over his body.

Rebecca was aware of the duke staring and had noticed his gaze lowering to her bodice; surely the length of time that his eyes had lingered was not appropriate for a man of his station, but she liked it. She liked the way it warmed her body. When she had gathered her senses, she thought that this could be fun; how she could fluster a man who was so impressive and masculine in every way that a woman desired. He was riled with his sister for some reason and now he might be a little upset with her for laughing.

He really needed to take the poker out of his you know what ...

Rebecca had been in his company for mere minutes, but she had met many gentlemen of the ton who behaved similarly. They expected young ladies to be seen and not heard, obeying them as if they were their property. She had to put up with this behaviour from her own brother and was not willing to sit back and watch her best friend's brother behave in the same way.

Rebecca had caught him looking at her in that way rakes did when she attended soirees, although when the duke looked at her, she had felt different; the tingling sensation between her thighs was unfamiliar, combined with the heat that she felt over her whole body. As he still stood in her way, Rebecca moved forward without thinking of possible consequences. She tilted her chin, looking him directly in the eyes, her arm brushing his as she passed, causing more of that new sensation to build in her core.

'Do you see something that is of interest to you, your Grace?' she whispered so only he could hear, her voice slightly breathless, before gliding into the room, aware of his gaze on her back, feeling the burn directly to her bones.

How satisfied Rebecca felt when she heard the low gasp from the duke. He had attempted to disguise the noise with the clearing of his throat - how she loved to shock the stuck-up members of the ton. Rebecca had become close friends with Lady Emma after an unlikely meeting at a ball. They had quickly bonded over a love of literature, particularly Gothic novels full of madness, eerie mansions and vampires. Another thing they had in common was that they both thoroughly enjoyed making mischief when the situation arose, and this had been one of these situations. Emma had spoken of her brother on many occasions, how pompous and dull he had become since his return with his new title. She also spoke fondly of a childhood that was filled with games and laughter, her brother joining in and at times teaching her new pranks to play on servants despite the age difference between them.

This was so far removed from her own childhood, growing up with siblings who were more concerned about appearances. Her brother, particularly, had always been the worst snob, and some of the behaviours he displayed were very immoral indeed. Rebecca also knew of the lewd pamphlets and literature he kept hidden beneath a floorboard in his study. She had gone in looking for him one morning and tripped up over the said floorboard. Curiosity getting the better of her, she lifted it and discovered his secret library. She only had a quick look as she feared Robert would catch her in the act and punish her severely.

Rebecca had enjoyed Emma's stories and had looked forward to meeting her dearest friend's elusive older brother on his imminent return, hopeful he would delight them with amusing tales from his travels. What she was not prepared for was the tall, muscular, brooding man who had stood in the doorway, his powerful presence causing her to blush. He wore no jacket, shirtsleeves rolled above his strong forearms, the shape of his broad shoulders straining beneath the white fabric of his shirt, the plain grey waistcoat he wore buttoned tightly over his taught stomach. Rebecca had to erase her thoughts, so she diverted them towards the tea tray, pouring herself a cup before her thoughts became any more improper. Her heart was beating so fast it felt as if it was about to burst out of her chest.

Is he still looking? Oh, my goodness, you do not blush Rebecca, and you must not allow yourself to lust over miserable, arrogant Dukes, even if he is so ...

Emma glanced over to Rebecca, interrupting her thoughts with a curious look. 'He is insufferable is he not, Rebecca, dear?'

All Rebecca could do was nod, as she lifted the teacup to her mouth, her heartbeat slowing at last.

Alexander had to take his leave NOW. His cock was so hard it would be difficult to conceal. Never had he been so aroused by the words of a lady, an innocent at that. The initial touch of her arm, as she brushed past him, had caused some excitement, but as soon as she opened her pouty lips and whispered those words, he had wanted to throw the little minx over his shoulder and march her to his bed chamber and discipline her so hard she would be screaming his name in pleasure. Imagining such a scenario was probably not wise in his current state. Mumbling a very quick good day, he took his leave and hoped that he wouldn't meet any of the servants in the hallway as he retreated to the solitude of his study.

CHAPTER TWO

~~~9♡♀~~~

TWO WEEKS LATER

'Brother, do you do anything for fun? I do not recall you leaving your study other than to eat dinner or break your fast. I believe that you may even sleep in there,' Emma said, folding her arms in exasperation.

'I have much work to do, sister,' Alexander replied without looking up.

Emma was not going to let things go that easily. 'But the sun shines, your grace. Let us take a walk. The ton speaks as if you do not exist. Many rumours surround your return and whereabouts,' she fretted.

Alexander did not care one bit what the ton thought. He had been called many things before he left; terms such as rake and libertine were most commonly used, alongside rumours that he had a gambling habit and drank to excess, of which much was untrue. Perhaps he had been a rake, but was that not how a young man behaved before he settled and took a wife? He was only flesh and blood after all. Like most hot-blooded males, he appreciated a beautiful face and form. He knew that he was very able when giving pleasure to a woman; he had been told as much on numerous occasions by the lonely widows and actresses that had shared his bed, both home and abroad.

The duke had dallied with many ladies, but rarely went back for more, preferring the chase, bedding them and moving on. He had taken several lovers over the years, always being honest that he couldn't offer them anything other than a night of passion.

Having grown up with parents who doted on one another, Alexander respected women and had always felt a sense of sadness that so many women of gentle breeding would never experience real pleasure or love with a man. The women of the ton were a perfect example of this, expected to lay back while the husband planted his seed before leaving to be with his mistress.

'Alex, Alexander, are you even listening to me? You do not even look up from those letters and ledgers. You do know that mother will be returning within the hour, and you know how she frets, especially since Papa has gone. If she suspects that you are hiding away from society, she will surely drag you to every ball, picnic and musicale by your shirt tails. She may even procure you a wife,' Emma gibed.

He couldn't help but laugh at his beloved sister; his mother the Dowager Duchess was a formidable presence. Scottish by birth, she had married the late Duke when she was two and twenty at a time when ladies were betrothed much younger and it had been a true love match. Evelyn Ainslie as she was known before marriage had many admirers, but refused them all, not caring when she was teased for being a spinster, regularly telling her children that she had been patiently waiting for their father and the evening that she first saw him across the ballroom she knew her wait had been worthwhile. Alexander and Emma would roll their eyes as they had heard this love story repeated on many occasions.

'Well, we cannot have mother grabbing my shirt tails, can we? That would be most un-dignified,' he retorted.

Alexander realised he had missed the company of his sister, and it would be no time at all before she would be wed and moments like this would become a rarity. Grinning to himself, he considered what poor gentleman would be enraptured by her but fail hugely trying to tame her wild spirit. He would never approve of a marriage that his sister was not happy with; she too deserved a love match.

The warm air hit Alexander as if he was back walking the streets of Florence. He screwed his eyes as they adjusted to the bright sunlight; it had been raining for several days, so there were still traces of muddy puddles on the cobbled roads. Not having ventured far from his study or chambers since arriving home, the noise of carriages and hooves was almost overwhelming. His thoughts drifted to the tranquility of the Italian landscapes and Spanish countryside, a longing that he couldn't contain, although he knew this was his life now, his destiny, his duty. Maybe after a few years, he could travel again, and explore some of the places he was yet to discover.

'Shall we venture directly to the park? Or we could partake in some sweet treats in those new tea rooms that I have heard so much about?' Emma smiled happily, thrilled that her brother was accompanying her rather than a maid.

'We can start with the park, and if you promise not to incessantly chat for the duration, I may be inclined to escort you for tea and cake,' he said.

Alexander offered his arm to Emma, gritting his teeth, dreading what was likely to be a showcase of fops, dandies, and eager young ladies wishing to be admired. Could this day get any worse? This was just the beginning of what was going to be a very long season.

~

Walking through the gates of the park, Alexander was not far wrong with his assumptions. Lovestruck couples promenaded with chaperones walking slowly behind. Gentlemen tipped their hats to passersby that they knew or recognised from their members' clubs and other less savoury establishments.

The Royal Park was vast, with sweeping lawns and wooded areas that homed hundreds of trees. There was an artificial lake used for boating in the summer months, where a dandy could impress a young lady with his rowing skills. Picnicking families sat by the Serpentine, shooing off local wildlife that dared to approach in the hope of getting scraps. Young Lords conversed in small groups, admiring the passing ladies who shielded their delicate complexions with frilly parasols and even frillier bonnets. As well as parading on foot, there was also the familiar sound of horses' hooves, the riders showcasing their finest clothes as they trotted down the avenue of Rotten Row.

This is ludicrous. It is as bad as I imagined.

The scene seemed idyllic to most, but he knew that it was also a place for vicious whispering, inappropriate behaviour from so-called gentlemen, and desperate mamas coercing their young daughters into the prospect of matrimony with every passing Lord, Earl or Marquis foolish enough to catch the older woman's eye.

'Is this not wonderful, brother? The sun is shining, and the most beautiful ladies and gentlemen of the ton are looking splendid in such fashionable attire.' Emma looked up at him with her contagious smile, the blue flowers of her bonnet enhancing the blue of her eyes. The same eyes that he too had inherited from their mother.

Alexander was aware that his sister was getting many admiring glances from young men as she walked at his side. He was also aware of the looks and whispers he was receiving from interested young ladies and curious men who didn't know whether to tip their hats or try to engage in conversation with the new influential Duke of Sandison. Leaving for the continent when he was but one and twenty, he never bothered corresponding with friends from his youth or University days, as many of them had also set off on adventures of their own.

Maybe it is time I became a member of a gentleman's club, and reintroduce myself to old friends, both socially and in business.

The duke knew that he had to ingratiate himself back into society, whether he wanted to or not. He could think of a few gentlemen from his youth that he would like to reacquaint himself with, hoping some familiar faces would make an appearance at the next ball, making the evening less tedious while chaperoning his sister.

So deep in his contemplations, Alexander had failed to notice that his sister had let go of his arm and dashed off. She was just a few steps ahead, chatting enthusiastically to a young lady wearing a lilac dress. The young lady who currently stood with her back to him was holding on to her bonnet as she threw her head back, laughing at something Emma had said. The dress she wore accentuated her slender waist and hung perfectly over her curvaceous behind.

I wonder if it hangs so perfectly in the front?

Alexander had not been with a woman since his return to London and was beginning to think he might need to remedy this situation soon, as it was not appropriate to be leering at innocents in such a public place with the eyes of the ton on him.

'Alexander, you remember my dearest friend, Lady Rebecca Rutherford?' Emma said as she gestured towards the young lady in lilac.

It is her again.

Of course, he remembered her, how could he not? The troublesome beauty had encroached on his thoughts several times over the past weeks, much to his dismay. Bowing, he greeted the young lady that he had been so vexed by previously. My lady.'

'Your Grace.' Rebecca curtsied, her flesh pinking as his eyes trailed lazily over the bare skin of her neck and chest. Gazing into those same eyes that had almost caused her knees to buckle a few weeks previous, she had forgotten the way he made her feel. She had put thoughts of him to the back of her mind, but here he was, so tall, so imposing, so handsome. So very handsome.

Breathe, Rebecca. He is just a man albeit a very ...... STOP.

Why did he have to look this good but be so arrogant and aloof? What else could she do to get under his skin, raise a smile from his perfect lips? She wondered.

'A fine day, is it not?'

His deep voice prompted a tingling sensation in areas that Rebecca had never imagined so sensitive. It was practically indecent standing next to the Serpentine while families were enjoying the good weather, wondering if the duke could relieve the ache. Thankfully, Lady Emma spoke, which eased some of the tension.

'It is quite the miracle that I convinced my brother to step outside at all, Rebecca. He seems determined to gain a reputation as a recluse.

Within the year, I am sure he will have a long beard and hair down to his knees!' Emma joked.

Smiling and feeling in the mood to irritate his grace once again, wanting to punish him for making her desire him when she did not wish to, Rebecca leaned into Emma, making sure that he would also hear her when she spoke.

'Oh, my goodness, Emma. How wonderful it would be to spend our afternoons braiding his grace's hair and tying bows and ribbons in his beard. He may even wish for some rouge. What do you think, your Grace? Pink or blue ribbon?' Rebecca added.

Emma was soon doubled over in laughter, picturing her brother's miserable face, his hair with ringlets and bows; he certainly did not have the same reaction, he was livid.

If looks could kill a person, Rebecca would not have lived another moment. She could barely contain her laughter, her rosebud lips snapping tightly shut, her eyes unable to hide the joy at seeing the look of anger on his face. Finally managing to compose herself and avoid any more stares from passersby, Emma fanned herself with her hand.

'Rebecca Rutherford, I do believe that you have rendered his grace speechless.' Emma continued to giggle as her brother looked at her with contempt.

'We must take our leave; I have much to do Emma. Come.' Alexander took his sister's arm in a more forceful way than he had done earlier, although careful not to cause her any pain. His face was flushed red, while his free hand hung by his side, his thumb unconsciously rolling over his signet ring.

Before saying their farewells, the young ladies arranged to correspond regarding something or other that Alexander had no interest in. Barely listening, doing the gentlemanly thing, he tipped his hat while offering a small head bob to Lady Rebecca, giving her the perfect opportunity to brazenly wink at him.

Did she just wink at me? Who is this creature? Is she deliberately trying to irk me?

As Rebecca rejoined her maid, they made off in the opposite direction with neither party looking back. Once again, she had managed to vex the duke. This was becoming quite an interesting hobby for her. After a very enjoyable morning, Rebecca made her way home, a skip in her step and a fluttering feeling in her belly. She was already contemplating her next move.

'Emma, I do not believe that Lady Rebecca Rutherford is a suitable person for you to keep company with. I find her to be more than a little disrespectful for a lady of her station,' Alexander spoke when they were out of earshot, failing to mention how his cock began to twitch at the mere thought of her luscious curves and sensual lips. Since the day they had first met, this woman had become the bane of his existence, with her witty little remarks. How he would delight in silencing that perfect impertinent mouth with his own.

'Brother, have you lost all sense of fun? We merely wanted to cause some mischief, and there is little all else to amuse us in this life that is mapped out from birth,' Emma sighed.

Alexander never knew his sister felt like this and he could not deny that she was correct. He really should be thankful that she was friends with ladies who wished for more than wealth and title, and who were not afraid to have opinions of their own and speak plainly. There was nothing worse than the insipid young ladies of the ton who took delight in spreading jealous gossip about their peers while parading the ballrooms of London.

'She is my dearest friend; she is the kindest, most generous, intelligent person I have ever known. Father said she was a joy to behold. He thought very dearly of her and her him. Did you know that in his weakest days, the two of us would read to him? He adored it when we took on the different characters from his favourite novels. And when Rebecca read him humorous poetry, he laughed so hard we thought he might burst!'

Alexander pondered this for a moment. Lady Rebecca Rutherford may have been the most irritating lady that he had ever met but now his interest was suddenly piqued, wishing to learn more. Being out of the country meant that Alexander had missed out on many things over the years. He found himself longing to know the life his father had lived in those years; forever grateful his life had been one of fulfillment and love. A similar life was all Alexander could ever wish for, albeit struggling at times to believe he would ever be deserving of the same life due to his somewhat nefarious past. But he would do his damnedest to ensure Emma did.

Not willing to forbid Emma from seeing her friend after these recent revelations, he would take great pleasure in keeping a close eye on things with Lady Rebecca Rutherford and her behaviour, convincing himself it was only out of brotherly concern for his younger sibling's reputation.

~

Rebecca Rutherford was the daughter of an Earl. As the youngest of four children, two of them sisters, she had enjoyed considerably more freedom than the older girls had been allowed. Her elder sisters were both married with growing families; the eldest, Rosalind was eight years her senior, and married to a Viscount, taking her duties as a Viscountess very seriously indeed. Rose had been born not more than twelve months after. She was sweeter in nature than Rosalind, wed to a Naval captain introduced to her by her sister's husband, Malcolm. Rose insisted the match had been love at first sight, she was currently anticipating the birth of her third child.

The two sisters both seemed sickeningly content in marriage which pleased Rebecca, but they were also critical of her behaviour at times, which they saw as unfitting for an unmarried lady of one and twenty.

The difference in ages meant that both sisters were married and beginning their new lives away from the family home when Rebecca was still a child. Although they visited on occasion, they had little time to entertain or converse with their younger sister. It was not until Rebecca came of age that they began to show interest, advising her on etiquette, how to style her hair and what dresses she should wear that would garner the attention of possible suitors.

Rebecca had longed for them to chat about less tedious subjects, trying to engage them in conversations about literature or art rather than what the ladies of Paris were wearing this season. Rosalind also took great pleasure in trying to play matchmaker at any given opportunity, whether it be a ball or dinner party, more concerned with title than who might suit her sister romantically. Although Rebecca was not averse to marriage, she would rather die a spinster than submit to a marriage of convenience with a penniless Lord who was more interested in her dowry. Then there was Robert, born five years before her, the heir. Robert was a very difficult man to like.

It had been quite the handful for the Earl, having four children. Their mother, his beloved wife, Mary had died from a terrible wasting disease when Rebecca was just four years old. She had very few memories of her mother and the family rarely spoke of her, her father finding it particularly painful. The Earl's heart had never healed, even after all the years that had passed; his dreams were haunted by the memory of watching the truest love he had ever known fade away before his very eyes.

The girls had been educated by a strict governess whose father had been a man of the clergy, insisting that they studied the Bible and lived to a high moral standard. Although stern in appearance and fanatical in her religious teachings, she would also show a much softer side when encouraging them to excel in reading and writing alongside French, music, and painting.

Rosalind outshone Rose in her languages, while the younger sister was more accomplished in painting and music. Rebecca's talents lay in writing. After she first realised a real passion for literature, she spent much of her time as a girl writing short stories and amusing rhymes about her siblings, much to their annoyance. It was not long before Rebecca fell in love with modern tales of monsters, ghosts, and hauntings, much to the governess's disapproval.

It was also important for young ladies to make polite conversation in company, which was far from Rebecca's greatest achievement! Ultimately, the young ladies of the household were being prepared for marriage, preferably to gentlemen of noble birth.

The heir, Robert was much easier for his father to deal with. As the male, he would be packed off to an elite boarding school when he was barely out of leading strings, set to mingle with more of his kind. Robert was but five years old when Rebecca was born, already being treated more favourably than his sisters, giving him that sense of entitlement that Rebecca hated.

Without a mother to shower her with love and a father so wrapped up in his grief, it was understandable that Rebecca would be a child who craved attention. It did not take her long before realising that she would get some of this desired attention by making mischief. Misbehavior would soon become Rebecca's favourite pastime, causing havoc for her governess and several tutors which led to much frustration for her father as she grew into womanhood. The Earl had little time or desire to tame this behaviour, expecting her to give up her foolish antics long before she came of age. This had been wishful thinking on his part.

Rebecca was seven and ten when her father passed away; the doctors had said his heart had stopped beating while he was out on a ride. There would always be rumours surrounding his death, with much speculation on whether he threw himself to his demise, unable to live another moment longer without his beloved wife. As was the way with the aristocracy, his body barely cold, Robert Rutherford was now the new Earl of Fordew at the age of two and twenty, a man too young to carry such power and responsibility, especially a man as reckless and irresponsible as her brother.

A year after the Earl's death with the required mourning period over, Rebecca was out in society attending her first ball of the season. At the grand old age of eight and ten, her brother was chaperoning her in the hope of finding her a husband. Arriving together but barely acknowledging the other's existence, Robert promptly left Rebecca in the company of a distant relative at the side of the ballroom, excusing himself before leaving to join the other men who would be playing cards that evening. The group of men that the Earl of Fordew associated with were quite renowned in the ton for betting obscene amounts of money during games, one young Lord having reportedly lost two thoroughbred stallions when his coffers had run dry.

It was at this very dull soiree when Rebecca was eight and ten that she first met Emma; moments after having boldly informed a young Lord that she could never court him due to his nose being so far in the air that a bird may mistake it for a tree branch.

Emma had heard the whole conversation and sniggered into her handkerchief. Thankfully, the older ladies who stood beside her failed to hear the insult due to the sound of the orchestra. They were also oblivious to any other goings on, engrossed in their own chat concerning some of the guests in attendance. When the deeply affronted Lord mumbled about never being so insulted and took his leave, Emma had spun round and taken Rebecca by the arm, guiding her to the refreshment area.

They had laughed and chatted for most of the evening, delighted that they both loved to read and discuss books, especially Gothic novels, which were considered unsuitable for young ladies who were expected to swoon at the mere mention of them. It was here on this night that Rebecca had finally found her first true friend, which made her happier than she had been for as long as she could remember.

~

Arriving home from her morning promenade, Rebecca handed her bonnet and gloves to Franklin, the family's loyal butler. Many of the servants had been with the family since she had been a babe, and many had been a victim of a trick or mishap involving her.

Rebecca was very close to her maid, Flora who had served all the Rutherford sisters until their respective marriages; the Earl was not willing to waste his coin on more staff than necessary when it came to the girls. Rebecca and Flora were inclined to gossip and giggle like old friends when out of earshot of other servants, an eye roll or stifled yawn would pass between them when they thought no one was looking.

This happened often when Rebecca was at an obligatory meeting with a potential suitor that had been set up by one of her siblings. She adored hearing the stories Flora told of her childhood, growing up in a close family that doted on each other. Even now, they all held a special bond, being openly affectionate and caring to one another. It was a simple life with little more than the love of family, but to Rebecca it was perfect. She had longed for her own family's love and attention for so long growing up, but now she realised the people who cared the most were her friends; her relations were purely a circumstance of her birth.

As well as purchasing the latest copies of the society scandal sheets on Rebecca's behalf, her loyal maid would collect books from the local bookseller, generally the Gothic novels that Rebecca devoured. The most recent book she had desired was currently still wrapped in brown paper in the bottom drawer of her desk, a Bible and some writing paper placed on top to hide it. Rebecca knew that it would be confiscated by her brother if found and replaced with some form of handbook detailing the flowers found in one's garden which he considered much more suited to a lady of her breeding.

Excited that she now had the book in her possession, Rebecca knew that she must make a start as the next meeting of the group was in three days. Unable to read her novel in any of the family rooms without being disturbed, she would have to feign a headache and forgo a proper dinner to allow her the space to absorb every word. So, with much eagerness to start reading the new book, Rebecca headed to her chambers for the rest of the day.

~

'You are lucky that I agreed to take you for tea and cake,' Alexander said to his sister while reaching for a scone.

Emma smiled over the rim of the teacup she had lifted to her lips. 'I always could get my way where you were concerned, dear brother.'

The duke raised an eyebrow before taking a sip of tea, 'You were a mere child then, sister. How could anyone have refused you when you looked like a chubby little cherub, with little fat hands pulling on my hair? Now that you are grown and no longer that child, you must begin acting like the young lady that you are, the spectacle that you made in the park, laughing like ... Heaven knows what.' He shook his head while wincing at the memory, 'With your insufferable little friend encouraging you, and all in front of the biggest gossips of the ton'.

Taking a moment to consider her brother's outburst before she spoke, Emma replied sharply. 'Since when did you ever bother what anyone thought Alexander? You never cared one bit about the whispers and rumours before you left. What has changed?'

'I do not care what they think of me, but I do care what they think of you Emma, now you are of marriageable age,' Alexander said.

Emma nearly dropped her teacup in surprise at her brother's mention of marriage. She never once considered that her beloved brother would be the one to thrust her into matrimony, even if she was more than aware that her position in society meant it was inevitable.

'Dearest brother, I never would have thought in my wildest dreams you would be so keen to rid me of your care so soon. We have not seen each other for so long, I would hate to think that you have become so terribly cold and uncaring that I could begin to compare you with poor Lady Rebecca's brother, the ghastly man will have her betrothed by the end of the season and will not bother whether the groom is twenty or ninety years. He could have not one hair on his head for all he cares, as long as he can provide a home for her away from him and his debauched lifestyle. The thought of her having to lie beneath such a man and produce his heir makes me feel quite unwell.' She squirmed.

'Emma, what do you know of such things?'

Alexander did not know whether to blush or laugh at her shocking outburst as he looked around ensuring that no one had overheard the conversation.

'Do not be so naive, brother. I am not completely unknowing of such matters. Many interesting conversations can be heard when standing near married ladies that have indulged in a little too much punch.'

Emma shrugged her shoulders before reaching for a biscuit. She and her friends regularly listened in on scandalous conversations at society events recounting what they had heard to each other.

Releasing a sigh, Alexander put his knife on his plate without finishing spreading the plum jam onto his scone. The mention of the irritating beauty's name caused him to look up, eager to know more about her and her own family. He had not been prepared for the shock he was now feeling after hearing his sister's words. It was not merely the fact that his sister knew of such things; it was the image of Lady Rebecca being bedded by any man other than him. He had forgotten how her beauty and annoying little quips had affected him since that first encounter some weeks previous.

Without wishing for his younger sister to suspect he had any interest in the little minx, Alexander suggested that the young lady's brother was quite right to insist on a favourable marriage for his unruly sister. This had not been his finest moment as he watched his sister clench her gloved hands, balling them into fists, her face red with anger.

'How dare you say such a thing. You do not even know her; you have met her twice and that was barely for a hello and goodbye.' Emma snapped.

Alexander responded to her with a groan; he was not going to bear witness to one of his sister's outbursts in public, although he could not help but admire her loyalty to her friend.

'You must admit, dear Emma, that on those two occasions, she was infuriating at the very least.'

What he wanted to say was that she was utterly captivating, and he could not get her out of his head. He recalled their first meeting in the hallway when she dared to whisper those enticing words, his gaze admiring the swell of her breasts, her creamy skin visible above the silk of her bodice.

'You can dislike the lady all you wish, your Grace, but that will not stop me from seeing her. She is my closest friend, after all. In fact, Rebecca will be joining me and some other ladies for tea later in the week.'

At that, Alexander returned to spreading the jam on his scone, suddenly ravenous and very much looking forward to seeing Lady Rebecca Rutherford again, curious as to whether their next encounter would be one of desire or disdain.

CHAPTER THREE

Although the book group was yet to find a suitable name, they had been meeting at Lady Emma's family home, once every month, for the past year. The ladies that attended all had a particular interest in Gothic novels, so these were generally the stories of choice for these gatherings.

This month had been Rebecca's choice, and she had devoured every page at least twice, the well-known author, Matthew Gregory Lewis being a favourite of hers. She often lost herself in the dark romanticism of his haunting tales, selecting an extract from her most prized novel that was kept hidden in her desk, having read it so many times the pages were creased and dog-eared.

The lady who selected each book had to rehearse a reading before performing it, much to the delight of the others present. The group was also an excuse for five friends to escape the tedious daily routines they had to endure as members of the ton, easily able to attend the meetings by telling their parents that they were having afternoon tea with Lady Emma Fane. This was never questioned due to her being the sister of a Duke, which was quite the kudos for their daughters, and favourable to their social climbing parents. This also meant that the meet-ups had to be held in the afternoons so as not to arouse suspicion, as the discovery of the literature they read would likely make the mamas swoon.

The ladies who were always in attendance were quite impressive in different ways and did not wish to conform to societal norms. Lady Matilda Brookfield was the daughter of a Duke and had been preened and prepped from a young age to enter society. A striking beauty with white, blonde hair and large blue eyes, she was the epitome of what was considered beautiful. With a wicked sense of humour and no desire to marry, the other young ladies agreed that she was the one who was most likely to be caught up in a scandal; possibly of her own doing.

Then there was Lady Katherine Paynter. Daughter of a Marquess, the physical opposite of Matilda in every way, her hair was a rich black. With a more curvaceous shape, she gave off a certain allure that made the younger gentlemen of the ton almost salivate whenever she stepped into a ballroom. Quite oblivious to the attention she received, she would happily stand in a corner observing the goings on around her rather than partaking in any courting rituals.

Lady Felicity Paynter was the cousin of Katherine and had been orphaned as a child when her parents had been tragically killed in a carriage accident. Felicity had been raised alongside her cousin and treated just like another daughter by the Marquess and Marchioness. Her father had been the younger brother of the Marquess, and they were very close growing up as young boys. Due to her parents' untimely death, Felicity was set to become a very wealthy woman when she turned one and twenty, which was only in another two years.

As attractive as her cousin but of slightly shorter stature, she would have no difficulty finding a suitor based on her countenance. But she was also aware that if news got out around the ton of her future inheritance, she would be hounded by unsavoury Lords with gambling habits aiming to compromise her to secure a chunk of her wealth.

Dismissing the servants when the tea and cake arrived, the five young ladies relaxed into their chosen seats, for the first time Emma had hosted them in the upstairs library which had confused the maids delivering the refreshments as she had never been known to use this particular room. There were none of the plush overly stuffed sofas, decorative cushions or freshly cut flowers that adorned the sitting rooms and parlours of the expansive townhouse, but the library furnishings were quite sufficient. Rebecca thought that the hard leather and darker colours of the masculine room were ideal for the ambience she wanted to create while telling this month's tale.

It was a sunny afternoon, the light shining through the floor-to-ceiling windows, causing Emma to squint slightly as she sat directly opposite. If only it was a dark evening the setting would be perfect, she thought.

'I am so excited to hear you read today, Rebecca. I know Mr Lewis's writings are your absolute favourite.' Felicity spoke with delight, removing her gloves and placing them on her lap. She settled into a more comfortable position now that it was just the five of them in the room, preparing to become engrossed in the afternoon's entertainment; if today's choice followed previous examples, they would become too immersed in the lurid literature to even ring for more cake.

'I am sure if he was still alive today you would be slightly in love with the great man himself,' Katherine added, which caused some laughter in the room. Rebecca answered by saying she was more in love with the characters in the novels than the man who created them.

'I do think we need more atmosphere in the room, to allow the story to come alive. I think I shall close the curtains, and a candle, yes, do you have a candle, Emma?' Rebecca was determined to put on quite the show for her friends.

Getting up, Emma crossed the room where she found a candle and tinderbox in the bottom drawer of the old ink-stained desk which had so many memories of her late father attached to it.

'Will these do? Father never liked candles to be lit in this room. He worried that it would cause a fire, and he would lose some of his precious books.' Emma's eyes glistened as she spoke of her late father when handing the items to Rebecca.

'I do hope his Grace will not scold you for disobeying your dear father's rules. I would hate for you to get into any trouble with your brother just because of me,' Emma said.

Rebecca's ponderings drifted off for a moment as she wondered how the Duke might scold her if she were to disobey him herself. She felt the heat building up in her face and a light fluttering in her belly as she imagined him backing her up against one of the bookcases before devouring her with his mouth.

'Rebecca, are you quite alright?' Her wicked thoughts were quickly diminished by Katherine's voice. 'You drifted off for a moment. I could have sworn you were going to faint. I have never seen you like that before, whatever is the matter?'

Rebecca's face flushed again as she felt embarrassed that she was caught thinking about the duke. 'I am fine now, thank you. I daresay that perhaps I ate that slice of fruit cake rather too fast, impatient to begin the tale,' she laughed. 'Let us continue now I am recovered.'

With the curtains now drawn, blocking out any daylight, the room was cast into darkness. The furnishings were crafted from rich woods and the imposing bookshelves were of similar colours. Even the spines of the leather-bound books matched the dark interior of the library, adding to the gloomy atmosphere.

'Oh, my goodness. I cannot even see my hand in front of me. Can you all say something so that I know you are still in the room,' Emma called out.

'I am still in the room,' Katherine answered at the same time as Matilda.

'Also, still in the room,' Felicity added clapping her hands with glee, 'How exciting is this? I hope you don't frighten us too much, Rebecca.'

Rebecca proceeded to light the candle which she then held aloft in the silver candlestick that Emma had fetched from one of the drawing rooms, the quivering aura illuminating her face, enhancing her delicate features. The stance gained her a round of applause from somewhere in the room, the darkness obscuring her audience.

'Good day, my dearest friends,' Rebecca projected her voice with a theatrical air. 'I tell the tale of temptation and lust.' The word lust encouraged a few sniggers in the darkness.

With the candlelight just shining bright enough for Rebecca to make out the silhouettes of her friends, she took a moment to remember the words that she had been rehearsing in the privacy of her chambers.

'It was the depth of winter: the night was already closing round us; and Strasbourg, which was the nearest town, was still distant from us several leagues.'

Rebecca recited the words in a quieter voice not much louder than a whisper, the candle flickering as she spoke. Although the ladies were now mere shadows in the room, she could hear the quickening of breath signalling that they were already engrossed in the famous tale.

~

Alexander had been informed by his sister that she would be taking tea this afternoon with the same ladies he had met previously. Unlike the last visit, the house was shrouded in silence, and he could not hear any feminine giggling or endless chatter. This was very strange indeed, as he knew that Emma would not have gone out without informing him.

Resting his elbows on the desk and looking straight ahead, unconsciously rubbing the ring that never left his little finger, his curiosity got the better of him. Standing up, stretching his arms in the air, he felt his neck clicking as he rotated his head to release some of the tension in the muscles. Alexander had been sitting at his desk updating ledgers and answering correspondence for most of the morning. There were days when he got so engrossed in his work he forgot to eat; his back would often hurt relieved only by a hot bath infused with lavender.

The open door revealed that the drawing room along the hall from his study was empty. The duke had expected to see his sister entertaining her friends; he wondered why he felt a wave of disappointment with the silence and the absence of a particular green-eyed beauty.

That is strange. What is my sister up to now?

The ladies had not uttered a word, they were so engrossed in Rebecca's tale as well as her acting skills.

'*The rain fell in torrents; it swelled the stream; the waves overflowed their banks ...*'

Rebecca continued to the conclusion of the story, her arms starting to ache from holding the candle aloft for so long.

Deciding that his sister was likely in the garden or her chambers, the duke continued with his day. Needing to retrieve some papers from his chambers, Alexander headed for the staircase. As he reached the top step, he was greeted with the sound of clapping and what appeared to be someone whistling. Increasing his pace, his long legs not needing to take more than five or six purposeful strides, he followed the noises which were emanating from the small library. The upstairs library had been his father's private space, full of rare and collectable books. When the previous Duke was in the room with the door closed, nobody was permitted to disturb him. The room was not out of bounds to the family, but it was rarely used since the Duke's death. Alexander stood for a moment listening at the door.

'My goodness, I still feel goosebumps on my skin. Matthew is just marvelous, Rebecca. I can understand why you are so enamored with him.'

The room was still only lit by the candlelight as Katherine was the first to congratulate her friend on her performance.

'I did tell you all that he is quite remarkable. He has the most fascinating mind and imagination,' Rebecca replied.

Alexander listened at the door. *Matthew, who is this man? I have never heard of anyone of that name.* He felt quite unsettled by the conversation he was hearing, question after question invading his brain.

Was the lady courting? Why were they in the library? Did the ladies want privacy to speak freely about things young ladies should not speak of?

'I am not sure that I would want to get too close to what goes on in his mind Rebecca, it seems to be rather dark,' Emma laughed.

Alexander would find out who this man was. He felt a slight anxious feeling in his chest, a feeling he had not experienced before. Was he jealous of a man he had never met? Visions of Lady Rebecca Rutherford whispering in the ear of another gentleman, tormenting him with her quips, made his gut ache.

His thoughts were instantly cut short at the sound of a yell, rustling of skirts, and stomping of feet. Without hesitation, he threw the door open to be greeted by utter darkness, the curtains drawn on what was a beautiful afternoon. Dashing to the window, he pulled open the heavy fabric, the sunlight drenching the room

'What is going on?!' he roared, noticing the four ladies and his sister taking a moment for their eyes to adjust to the light.

'Brother! All is fine. Just a little accident, an overreaction. Nothing to concern yourself with. You may leave us.' Emma could not have looked or sounded more guilty.

'Is that burning? I can smell burning! Something is burning?' Surveying the room and the ladies in it, his eyes searched for Rebecca. Standing to the side of the others, her hair had come loose from its braid, her cheeks were slightly flushed. Wearing a simple gown of pale blue, Alexander could not help but admire how the silk clung to her ample breasts, the visible milky skin above her décolletage rising and falling as her breath began to quicken when she noticed him staring.

Reluctantly removing his eyes from her heaving breasts, Alexander followed Rebecca's gaze, which was focused on her feet, immediately tucking one behind the other when she saw him looking.

'Why does the lady wear only one shoe?' he queried, directing the question to his sister.

'Do not be angry with Rebecca. We are all at fault, brother. The candle fell and landed on the floor, but Rebecca extinguished it quickly with her foot.' Emma crossed over to where her brother stood and gently patted him on the arm as she tried to appease him.

'We will discuss this later; you know that candles are not permitted in this room Emma, what were you thinking?' He tried to keep his voice low and remain calm in the presence of the ladies who were now looking incredibly awkward, when he heard a quiet snigger.

'Do you find something amusing, my Lady?' Alexander did not even have to look up as he knew who found this whole scenario so humorous.

'I am so sorry, your Grace. I often laugh when I am nervous, and I stand before you in one shoe that now has a hole burnt into the sole.' Rebecca held her shoe up to show the room the damage, noticing the thunderous look on the duke's face and the way he fidgeted with the signet ring he wore.

'Rebecca, are you alright you could have received a nasty burn,' Katherine chipped in.

'Oh my, is it painful?' Felicity worried.

'Shall we call for a physician?' Emma gasped.

Casting a side glance at Alexander, Rebecca lifted the hem of her dress slightly, revealing more of her leg than was socially acceptable in front of a gentleman. 'I very nearly did Katherine, look how my shoe has melted, and will you look at the little hole in my stocking foot.'

Rebecca discussed the incident with her friends as if the duke was not even in the room, much to his irritation. None of the other ladies were in the slightest bit shocked at Lady Rebecca's behaviour; Alexander, on the other hand, could not believe what he was seeing. He had noticed that she had glanced over at him before the display and was sure it was for his benefit, more than aware that she enjoyed trying to vex him. That glance at her shapely ankle and the tiniest piece of flesh visible through the damaged silk made his mouth go dry. He had to tear his eyes away from the scene unfolding as he felt his member begin to twitch, imagining how it would feel to remove the ruined stocking, and trail kisses up the smooth skin of her leg before reaching the apex between her thighs.

His wicked thoughts were quickly extinguished as he was forced to listen to the prattling voices suggesting how a person might mend the stocking, and whether or not she could wear the shoe home without suffering her brother's wrath. As Emma watched her brother's expression become more and more surly. She knew he was getting increasingly irritated by the whole situation, meaning he would be in a dreadful mood for the rest of the day. Summoning a footman, she hastily arranged for carriages to be brought around and bid Katherine, Matilda, and Felicity a fond farewell as they all agreed to meet up soon.

Alexander fled the room before he said or did something that he might regret. The ladies of the ton that he was acquainted with did not behave like these ladies. He would need to chat with his sister; how would she find a suitable husband associating herself with the likes of Lady Rebecca Rutherford? Rebecca Rutherford was the most annoying, troublesome, stunningly beautiful creature he had ever met.

'I am sorry if I caused you strife with his Grace.' Rebecca genuinely felt guilty at the thought of her friend suffering her brother's anger. 'Sometimes it is like a little goblin takes over my reasoning. It has been this way since I was a little girl.'

'Oh, my dear Rebecca do not apologise, it is what makes you who you are, although I must admit the look on Alexander's face when you revealed the hole in your stocking will be worth whatever punishment I receive.' She chuckled.

'Oh dear, he will not punish you severely, will he?' Rebecca was deeply concerned at what the Duke may do to chastise Emma, familiar with severe treatments, having received many at the hands of her brother. She had been locked in dark rooms, and much-loved books were thrown in the fire; once he had even held her down, washing her mouth with soap because she dared answer him back.

'No, he will just threaten me with marriage,' Emma laughed. 'He may come across as stern and a little terrifying, but he would do anything to protect me and anyone else that he loves. He is a kitten, really. Now, I will not be a moment while I go fetch you a pair of my shoes. You cannot be travelling home in the one shoe.'

Rebecca was thankful that they wore the same shoe size. If her brother Robert was to catch sight of her arriving home wearing just one shoe, she would be married off to some fat old Lord by the following week. As she waited for Emma to return, Rebecca sat down to remove the other shoe. Leaning back, she closed her eyes, enjoying the silence of the room before stretching her legs out in front of her. Rebecca considered how she would never be allowed the freedom in her own home of relaxing in such a way, she looked down at her feet and gently wiggled her toes, the movement causing the hem of her dress to rise slightly revealing her slender calves.

'Do you deliberately go out of your way to torment me, my lady' The deep masculine voice came from the direction of the open doorway startling her so much that she let out a tiny shriek.

Rebecca was greeted by the sight of the Duke of Sandison standing in the open doorway, his arms folded across his broad chest. He was glancing at her stocking-clad feet which were clearly visible, Rebecca quickly pulled down the hem of her dress, rearranging her skirts, the duke's eyes never once straying from the scene he was witnessing.

'Oh, my goodness you gave me quite the fright, your Grace,' she said.

Rebecca could feel her heart racing as their eyes eventually met and the heat radiating through her body. Unable to take her eyes off him, she was determined not to blush while admiring his confident strides as he made his way towards where she sat. Rebecca had never felt nervous in the presence of anyone like she did right now. He was so incredibly handsome, his black hair rakishly flopped over his forehead which he quickly swept back revealing more of his beautiful, chiselled face; the dark stubble visible on his chin made him look more dangerous, if not more enticing.

Managing to compose herself, Rebecca got up from the chair, hoping she would feel less intimidated by his nearness. Her heart began to beat faster as his eyes gazed openly at the rise and fall of her chest. Rebecca began to back away, deliberately creating some distance between them before she realised she had backed herself into a corner. Rebecca had never been alone with a gentleman before who was not her brother, certainly not one that she was so attracted to, a man who also smelt divine. Rebecca was sure she could smell lavender emanating

from him as he stood so close to her, she wondered if this was unusual for a man as her brother mainly smelled of tobacco and spirits.
Men just use plain soap do they not? Does he use lavender soap? How interesting.

After Rebecca's most recent behaviour, Alexander suspected that she would expect him to ignore her before walking away, his angry eyes boring into her with a look of contempt. If only she knew the looks from him were not of anger, but overwhelming desire and lust. Standing before her, he felt a twitching in his breaches as he recalled the way her skirts had risen revealing beautiful, shapely ankles. In that moment he had wanted nothing more than to lift her dress, inch by inch, to reveal more of her legs, until his hands rested against the bare flesh of her thighs. Then Alexander would show her what happened to insolent young ladies.

Not many words had been spoken since Alexander had entered the library. They had both just looked at each other, each waiting for a reaction of some sort from the other. Silent but for the sound of her breaths, Rebecca made to move past him, not wanting to be caught in what could be seen as a very compromising situation. She was no vixen or hoiden; she had done nothing more than kiss a stable boy out of curiosity when she was five and ten, recalling that it had felt quite pleasant, if not rather wet.

Still fearful that Emma could appear at any given moment and the situation she now found herself in, Rebecca foolishly remained where she was. Alexander was now towering over her; he was so close that she could see different shades of blue in his eyes perfectly framed with thick black eyelashes. The smell was most certainly lavender. Both had now locked eyes with each other; Rebecca let out a barely audible gasp as she watched him run his tongue along his bottom lip.

Is he going to kiss me? No, he must not kiss me. I want him to kiss me.

Her thoughts conflicted; she couldn't take her eyes off him. His towering presence now caging her against the wall in the corner of the room. The door was open slightly, Rebecca hoped that she would hear if anyone approached allowing time to add some distance between herself and the duke. The room had suddenly become warmer, he was so close to her now, she could feel the heat emanating from his body.

Alexander was almost overcome with desire; inhaling the smell of her hair, a floral scent he could not quite place, her skin up close was like porcelain with a few tiny freckles on the bridge of her nose. Her lips were slightly parted which was when he noticed the slight gap between her front teeth. How had he failed to notice this unique part of her natural beauty? She would drive him to distraction; she was the bane of his life. He must not take this further than he had planned, it was on a whim that he decided to cause a little mischief of his own. When he had walked past the open door and saw her sitting by herself looking all innocent, he had decided to play her at her own game.

'Your Grace, what are you doing? This is highly improper.' Trying not to sound breathless when he leaned in closer, his lips gently brushing her neck, she willed herself not to sigh and reveal how his presence was affecting her.

'You enjoy playing games, *Rebecca*?' The way he whispered her given name into her ear while his lips grazed the lobe caused a warm sensation in her belly. 'We can all play games *Rebecca*,' he growled.

Alexander knew he was getting the right reaction as his body caged her within the confines of the room. He desperately wanted to plunge his tongue into her beautiful mouth while his fingers explored the dampness between her thighs, but this was about games, and the best game for him to play was to leave the lady wanting.

Without moving, his hands firmly placed on the wall at either side of her head, the duke moved his lips closer. She began leaning forward in the anticipation of a kiss. Alexander had never wanted to kiss someone more in his life. His arousal was almost painful, but he needed to control his urges for the long game that he had in mind. In an instant, before he could reconsider, Alexander removed his arms before he succumbed to her lips. He knew that one kiss would never be enough; he could sense a passion in Rebecca that had yet to be explored and when that passion was released neither of them could go back. They were not right for each other; she would drive him to distraction with her uncouth behaviour and smart little mouth.

That mouth. What I could teach her to do with that mouth...

Moving to the side, allowing her space to free herself, Alexander now focused his attention on looking out of the window to the gardens below. He refused to look at her perfect face and what was likely a look of confusion at what had transpired in those last few minutes.

'You may leave. Emma has ordered you a carriage and she will give you a pair of shoes to wear home.'

Turning around he glanced at where she stood, a tantalising stockinged foot slightly visible from beneath the hem of her gown. His voice was cold and abrupt, unlike the husky tempting tone he had used previously.

Rebecca's initial look of confusion quickly turned to one of anger as she gathered her skirts while marching across the room. The scene would have been comical if there had not been so much tension in the air. In her hastiness to leave, she had put on the undamaged shoe which caused her to walk in the most ungraceful way, carrying the burnt one as she fled. Never one to be defeated, she knew she must have the last word. Rebecca took a moment while she gathered herself before turning to where the duke was now standing, his back to her while he absentmindedly fidgeted with his father's ring, something that he did when he was nervous or anxious.

Does she make me nervous?! A lady has never made me nervous.

'I know you want to kiss me your grace but just so you know,' she paused before taking a deep breath. 'You will never, ever experience the feel of my lips against yours, EVER.' She then left him to his thoughts before forcefully pulling the door behind her.

Alexander was more turned on than he had ever been with her little performance. His arousal had begun to subside but when she said the word kiss and then *'never experiencing the feel of her lips,'* he was instantly as hard as a rock again. He would need to wait a few moments until the bulge in his trousers had gone down before leaving the room.

This is just the beginning of the games my beautiful little firecracker. You will be begging for me to kiss you before the month is out.

Alexander had to admit to himself that it was not going to be easy to stop himself from seducing the lady the next time he had her alone, but all in good time.

~

Rebecca was now settled in the carriage; Emma had come down the stairs with the shoe seconds after she had slammed the door on the duke. She was grateful that her friend had not questioned why she was standing waiting in the hallway, the door behind her firmly shut.

Her heart had raced at the thought that she could have been caught in a very compromising situation indeed if her friend had returned moments before. The room had been so full of tension, that it would be obvious to any third party that something had transpired between them in the short time they were alone. The duke's desire was more noticeable than hers, something a sister would most definitely not want to witness in a brother.

Rebecca was glad to be getting away as quickly as possible, annoyed with herself for allowing Alexander Fane to take such liberties, also ashamed that she had allowed her desire to overtake any reasoning, the duke now knowing that she was not unaffected by him. Rebecca was positive that he had wanted to kiss her. She could feel the heat radiating through the fabric of his clothes, the blue of his eyes darkening as he stared at her with a longing that suggested he wanted to devour every inch of her body if she would let him. Rebecca was not sure if she could have resisted him at that moment in time and may very well have let him.

Although an innocent, she knew what it meant if a man had a growing bulge at the front of his trousers and had been more than aware of something hard brushing against her hip as she felt his warm breath against her ear.

CHAPTER FOUR

As the carriage arrived at her home, a footman stepping forward to help her down, she felt a sense of relief at the slight breeze on her face. She had been quite hot from the journey, still reeling from what had happened with the duke in the library. Walking through the front door, laying down her bonnet and removing her cloak, her maid, Flora appeared looking flustered, a slight frown on her normally cheerful face. Rebecca prepared herself for what was to come, suspecting it concerned her brother, the Earl.

'Is something amiss, Flora?' moving forward Rebecca lifted one of the maid's hands, noticing that she was shaking. 'Whatever is wrong?'

Flora took a moment; she looked around to see if anyone was about before placing her other hand over Rebecca's.

'Your brother requests you join him in his study on your return. He has been looking for you all day, my lady,' Flora continued to speak in a quieter voice so none of the other servants could hear the conversation. 'He has a gentleman I do not recognise in his study. His lordship was behaving like a madman, slamming doors, and shouting your name up until the gentleman arrived.'

The maid knew that she was able to speak to her mistress in a way no other servant could, especially when it concerned the Earl who she despised.

'I was unaware of any visitors calling today. Do you know the gentleman's name?' Rebecca queried.

'No, my lady. He could be a business associate I suppose but due to his advancing years, it is unlikely they are university friends,' Flora stated.

Rebecca suddenly felt overcome with nausea. She knew it was only a matter of time before the Earl would offer her hand to someone of his acquaintance, beneficial to him and his future plans, with no consideration to her feelings. She feared that the gentleman who now awaited her arrival in the room just along the hallway must be here for her; why else would her brother be frantically trying to locate her?

It had only been a few days ago that she had accidentally dropped a book in the library, failing to notice her brother Robert was sleeping on a chair in the corner. The thudding of the book as it hit the floor had woken him from his alcohol-induced slumber, his words slurred and almost incomprehensible, not even bothering to open his eyes. He had mumbled, 'The sooner you are off my hands and are some other poor bastard's problem, the better.' Rebecca had not cried or been hurt by his comments, she had actually stifled a laugh at his course language and the slurring of words.

Suddenly, heavy footsteps could be heard making their way towards where Rebecca stood chatting with Flora, the hurried sound sending a sense of panic through her as she prepared to be scolded by her brother. The Earl of Fordew had a vicious tongue; he would often chastise the younger female servants over the slightest mishap. Rebecca had seen many a young maid in floods of tears after being reprimanded for one petty thing or another. She could only give them a pitying look as Robert was the master of the house, although Rebecca had managed to secure a position with another household for one particular young maid who had been constantly bullied by the Earl, causing her much distress.

'Sister, I see you have decided to return?' Robert peered at her with bloodshot eyes, the smell of brandy on his breath, looking her up and down, a look of judgment on his sneering face.

'You are coming with me this instance.'

'Coming where?' she asked, knowing fine well where they were going.

'Do not be insolent. I have a guest who wishes to make your acquaintance, so you will put a smile on that miserable face and act like the lady you are supposed to be.'

'Who is the caller? Is it a gentleman? Do I know of him?' Rebecca thought she would delay her brother by asking more questions for her amusement.

How dare he make such demands of me.

'That is of no concern to you. Now, come with me immediately.' His hands fisted by his sides as he spoke, his knuckles turning white.

Before Rebecca could open her mouth to speak, she felt the strong grip of her brother's hand around the top of her arm, so hard that she knew it would leave a bruise. Rebecca often had marks or bruising to her body, always done in such a way that any traces of punishment would be hidden beneath her clothing.

'You are hurting my arm, Robert, please let me go,' Rebecca spoke quietly as she did not want the servants to hear her pleading voice, as they were known for gossiping.

When they reached the study Robert released her arm, it was throbbing from the pressure, so she began rubbing it to soothe the pain, her eyes glistening with tears that never came.

'Now, I am warning you to behave. This is *important* to me.' His bloodshot eyes were now practically bulging out of his sweating head.

Rebecca instantly knew what this meant; she soon felt another wave of nausea combined with a feeling of panic that this was to be the moment she had feared the most. She was about to meet her future husband for the first time.

The Earl proceeded to walk into the room, his sister following at his back, the sound of silence deafening. Rebecca could not see over her brother's shoulder as he stood more than a foot taller, the smell of pipe smoke almost making her retch. Composing herself, she nervously clasped handfuls of her skirts before she was presented to the stranger in her midst.

Robert Rutherford cleared his throat as he stepped to the side, indicating to Rebecca to move forward. A gentleman stood in the centre of the room, a glass containing a dark liquid in his hand.

'Lord Phillips, may I introduce my sister Lady Rebecca Rutherford.' Robert discreetly nudged her in the direction of the lord.

'Rebecca, Lord Phillips,' Robert took a step back, allowing Rebecca to step forward, before offering a slight curtsy.

As the Lord was introduced, she felt uncomfortable with more than a hint of embarrassment when his eyes roamed over her body, a very different reaction to the one she felt with the duke earlier in the library.

His countenance was not wholly unattractive, albeit he was at least thirty years her senior. His fair hair was showing signs of white at the temples and he looked as if he had the beginnings of a small paunch straining against his waistcoat. However, he was tall and had a fine head of hair for his advancing years, she supposed. Her thoughts once again strayed to that of the duke, with his black hair, flat stomach and muscular thighs, soon snapping back to reality when the man began to speak.

'Lady Rebecca, at last. I was beginning to think you were avoiding me. I must say, it was worth the wait. You are more exquisite than I could have imagined.'

Rebecca felt as if ants were crawling on her skin at each word he spoke. Robert was watching the interaction carefully, waiting for her to say or act in the wrong way.

'Lord Phillips has travelled from Kent to meet with you sister. He wishes to make your acquaintance before Lord and Lady Strathdee's ball.'

Rebecca nodded and smiled, although she felt like screaming when a maid entered the room to announce that tea was ready to be served in the parlour. She could not fail to notice the way the Earl looked at the young maid in a similar way he had her not ten minutes before.

'Let me escort you, my lady,' Lord Phillips offered his arm as they headed towards the parlour.

The two men did most of the talking while they took tea, the conversation of little or no interest to Rebecca; several times she had to stifle a yawn. She had tried to engage the man in conversation by asking questions concerning literature, art, and even horses but he showed no regard for any of the topics and returned to conversing with her brother.

At long last, she noticed him looking at his pocket watch, signaling that he was about to leave. Rebecca wanted to let out a sigh of relief; it had been the longest hour of her life. She did not even mind when he brushed his thin lips over her knuckles in farewell, as long as it signified he was leaving. There was something about Lord Phillips that made her feel unsettled, although she could not quite put her finger on it. What was all of this for? Was he planning on courting her or had her brother promised her hand in marriage? The meeting was now over, and she was still none the wiser.

'Robert, how do you know Lord Phillips? I have never known you to speak of him?'

'He is a very wealthy investor with many business interests. He now seeks a wife who can help advance his place in society as well as provide him with an heir. That is all you need to know.'

'But what do you know of his character? I do not know if I like him,' Rebecca protested.

'That is of no significance to me, sister. If he decides after the ball that you suit, you shall be married within the month.' Pushing past her, he left the room, keen to return to his half-empty bottle of brandy.

~

Rebecca was back in her bed chamber. She had decided to pen a letter to her friend, Emma and now sat at her writing desk, so angry and upset that she needed to vent her frustrations in some way, secretly hoping her dearest friend would help her out of this current predicament. It was not unusual for the friends to send each other notes. It was an easier way to share secrets and discuss the next novel they would read before the book group than discussing it in public. It was also a convenient way to communicate due to them all living nearby to each other, meaning urgent letters could be received quickly. They also had a pact that they must throw any correspondence in the fire after reading, destroying any evidence of misbehaviour.

It had been decided that Emma would always be the main recipient of any letters as she did not have the type of relations that might intercept her personal correspondence. It was likely that one of the other young ladies would be exposed by a nosey parent or sibling who took pleasure in knowing their private business.

After considering her words for a moment Rebecca decided to keep her note short and straight to the point.

My Dearest Emma

I had to write to you as soon as I could, as I feel my life as I know it may be over.

Today when I returned home after such a wonderful afternoon with my dearest friends, my worst nightmare may have come true. Robert had been in the foulest of tempers, behaving like a mad man according to Flora. The reason for his foul mood was that he had arranged for a gentleman to call on me and I was not at home. The gentleman is known as Lord Phillips and is surely old enough to be my father. He is to attend the Strathdee ball with us, and I fear that my brother may announce our engagement.

I cannot marry him; I do not know him; I do not like him.

Emma, what must I do?!

I shall call upon you tomorrow at noon and tell you everything. If you can inform M, K and F of my predicament they may have some thoughts on how I can be saved from a life of misery.

Rebecca

Sealing the note, Rebecca went in search of Flora who would discreetly pass the letter to a footman, who would walk or ride the short journey to Emma's home, delivering it safely. As this was a regular occurrence, the servant would be aware that he did not need to wait for a written reply; also under Flora's instruction, the Earl must never know of their mistress's correspondence. The footman was more than happy to oblige as the Earl was an unpopular figure in the household, while Rebecca was well-liked amongst the servants.

CHAPTER FIVE

Alexander was trying to concentrate on reading the papers in front of him, but his thoughts kept drifting back to Lady Rebecca Rutherford. Leaning back in his chair, the memory of how she reacted to the closeness of his body in the library, caused the beginnings of a smile to form on his lips.

'Alexander Fane, are you smiling?' Evelyn Fane stood in the doorway looking suspiciously at her son.

'I did not know you were home. Did you have a pleasant journey?' Alexander stood up to greet his mother.

'Good, thank you, dear. Your aunt sends her regards and asks if you have found yourself a wife yet. Have you found yourself a wife?' With a mischievous look on her face, Evelyn knew how her son became irked at the mere mention of marriage.

'I am not yet thirty, mother. I have plenty of time to find a suitable Duchess. I have no need of an heir just yet,' he grumbled.

The Dowager Duchess seated herself on the chair opposite Alexander's desk, smoothing the skirts of her black gown.

'I think we should be more concerned with Emma procuring a suitable husband, mother. Her behaviour is somewhat questionable at times for a lady of her breeding.'

Evelyn let out a loud laugh as she clapped her hands in amusement.' My dear boy, your sister will meet someone of her own choosing when the time is right. I will not allow anything other than a love match for her, as I had with your father. You may now be the duke, but that is one thing that I will not allow you to interfere with. You would not want to see your sister living an unhappy, unfulfilled life. She is much too spirited, and you know it'.

Alexander was not going to argue with his mother. He knew she was right, but society still believed young ladies of the ton should be matched to gentlemen of suitable rank and family connections. Love matches were still incredibly rare. When the time was right, he would be looking for a lady of impeccable breeding to play the role of Duchess.

'You are home', Emma skipped into the room, delighted to see her mother returned from her extended visit to her elder sister's home in the Scottish Borders. Leaning down, she kissed her mother on the cheek before settling herself on the small sofa.

'I am trying to work; I have much to do.' Alexander was slightly irritated that both ladies had joined him in his study, not looking as if they were planning on leaving anytime soon.

His mother got up from her chair, but rather than leaving, joined her daughter on the sofa.

'We are not stopping you from working. Imagine we are not here, brother,' Emma said.

How can I pretend you are not here when you are sitting chatting and laughing not a stone's throw from me?

A short time passed. His mother and sister were still deep in conversation. Attempting to absorb the huge pile of paperwork in front of him, he looked up as the butler knocked before entering the open door.

'Apologies for the interruption your Grace, a letter has arrived for Lady Emma,' the butler announced.

Emma quickly got to her feet, took the letter, thanking the butler as he bowed leaving the room as quickly and discreetly as he had appeared. Recognising the handwriting, Emma wondered why she would be receiving a letter from her friend as they had seen each other earlier that day.

'Is everything alright dear, you look a little surprised at receiving the letter?' Evelyn asked.

'I do hope so, mother. The handwriting is Rebecca's, although we saw each other not four hours ago. I do not understand why she would write so soon.'

Alexander's ears soon pricked up as Rebecca's name was mentioned. He had not been paying much attention regarding the letter his sister had received as it was not his business to pry. Looking up from his work, he was now very much interested in the conversation between mother and daughter.

'I am sure it is nothing to concern yourself over Emma. She must have forgotten to mention something or perhaps she has some exciting news from her journey home, you know how excitable the girl gets,' her mother said trying to reassure her youngest child.

Emma nodded, hoping her mother was correct in her assumptions, then proceeded to unseal the letter.

Keen not to draw the attention of his mother, Alexander anxiously watched his sister's expression as she began to read. Surely, Rebecca would not be writing to tell her friend what had transpired earlier

41

between them in the library. Emma suddenly let out a short gasp before covering her mouth with her hand and shaking her head.

'No, no, no this cannot be allowed to happen,' Emma cried.

Alexander selfishly felt some relief that this was some other matter and not what he had feared. Although keen to know what had caused his sister to react in such a way.

'Lord Rutherford is forcing Rebecca into an arranged marriage with some older gentleman. Lord Phillips is his name.'

'Oh, poor darling Rebecca, she does not deserve this.' the Dowager comforted her daughter by placing a hand on her arm.

'Oh, mother! She fears there is to be an announcement of their engagement at the Strathdee ball this coming week.' Emma wept.

Evelyn had a look of pity in her eyes as she looked at her daughter and then at her son, a reminder of the conversation that they had earlier about marriage.

'Do you know of Lord Phillips, Alexander? It is not a name that I have heard of before?' Emma asked.

'Not sure that I have, but I *have* been out of the country. I can ask about it if you wish me to. I shall be meeting some associates at Whites this evening, thought it was wise to form some alliances with my peers, although having to listen to some of them prattle on is hardly worthy of the fees,' Alexander griped.

As soon as the man's name was mentioned, Alexander had decided that he would find out who he was, whether he was asked to or not. The bastard was not going to get his grubby hands on her. Alexander had just gotten started with the games he had planned, Lady Rebecca Rutherford his beautiful little distraction from his ducal duties. He had never known jealousy before, presuming this might be what he was experiencing. The thought of another man's name spoken from her lips as he pleasured her perfect body made the duke's blood boil. She had captivated him in a way no other woman had, and he didn't know if he loved or loathed it.

'She is coming to call tomorrow at noon, so I must invite Katherine, Felicity and Matilda to join us.' Getting up from the sofa, Emma stayed true to her promise and threw the letter into the fire as she left the room.

'I presume you have met the enchanting Lady Rebecca?' The Dowager stood as she posed the question to her son.

'I have, briefly, on three separate occasions,' he replied.

'Mm-hmm. You seemed very interested in her predicament. The colour drained completely from your face when your sister read the letter, and as for that poor balled-up piece of parchment you are still crushing in your hand ...'

Exiting the room, he knew she had a smile on her face. A more intuitive person he had never met.

CHAPTER SIX

As the new Duke of Sandison, it was imperative he associated himself with a prestigious gentlemen's club. His father had been a member of Whites, and the elite establishment was delighted to welcome him as a member. The club was exactly as he had anticipated, gentlemen sat around lazily drinking spirits, reading the news sheets and playing cards. Some tables were rowdier than others as bets were won and lost with patrons cheering and mocking each other.

Alexander took a seat in the corner farthest away from the more inebriated clientele, a whisky promptly set in front of him by the passing waiter. About to take his first sip, he was startled when he felt the weight of a large hand on his shoulder.

'Alexander Fane, I thought that was you, or should I say …. Your grace?' the man declared.

It took a minute before Alexander recognised the gentleman that stood before him; the self-assured smile and unruly hair gave him away although several years older and several inches taller than when they had last met.

'Bloody hell, Benjamin Turner! How long has it been?'

'Too long, I am sure. How have you been?'

Ordering more whisky, the two men began to catch up on what they had been doing in the ten years since they had last seen each other. They had been firm friends at boarding school before going to different universities.

As they recalled some of the escapades they had gotten up to as young boys, their conversation was interrupted by the sound of angry shouting from across the room where a small group of younger Lords had gathered. There was a sound of breaking glass then all hell broke out. Some of the older men ran over and were holding back a very drunk young man, his eyes full of rage as he struggled to free himself.

'You are a fucking cheat and a thief, Montrose', the drunk man snarled as he was steered toward the exit.

'You are a bad loser, Rutherford. I won fair and square,' Montrose retorted.

'You are a liar; you were hiding bloody cards,' the drunk man snarled back at him.

'How dare you accuse me of such a thing. You lost again, Rutherford. I doubt you have anything else to stake if rumours serve me correct?'

The response from the man named Montrose obviously resonated with the Earl as he made a growling noise before trying to swing for him, only to be held back by an older gentleman who was trying to calm him while escorting him towards the club's exit.

'Come now, you do not want to make this any worse for yourself, my Lord. Go home and sleep it off,' the white-haired man pleaded.

After another violent exchange between the two young men and several threats from the man that Alexander now knew as Rutherford, things eventually began to calm down. There was a little more pushing and shoving before he was finally removed from the premises and deposited in a carriage home. Alexander could not help but feel sympathy for whoever he was going home to, whether it be a wife, sister or mother.

The club soon returned to respectability, everyone continuing as if nothing had happened, Alexander and Benjamin sat back down, each taking a swig of whisky before allowing a fresh measure to be poured.

'Is it always this riotous?' Alexander asked.

'Only when Robert Rutherford is in his cups and gambles away more of his family's coffers,' Benjamin answered.

It took a moment before Alexander realised. 'Is Rutherford the same Rutherford as in the Earl of Fordew?' Alexander wanted the answer to be no but knew it was unlikely.

'The very same. Why do you ask?'

'His sister is very good friends with my sister, Emma. She had mentioned him to be unpleasant and now I have witnessed that first hand.'

'So, you have met the delightful Lady Rebecca Rutherford? She kicked me in the shins once when I asked her to take a stroll in the gardens with me at a ball last year.' Benjamin laughed at the memory, not failing to notice the scowl on his friend's face.

'I apologise, your grace. I did not mean to offend; I had no idea you and the lady were ...'

'You do not offend and do not call me that. I am Alexander or Fane, whichever you wish. I find the title can be quite suffocating. Also, there is nothing between myself and the lady. She drives me to distraction every time we meet, she is so, so ... brazen'

'But also very beautiful, do you not agree?'

Alexander could not disagree with that but was not going to admit to a friend he had not seen for years that she was constantly in his thoughts.

'Talking of Lady Rebecca and her tyrant of a brother, I need to ask you something before I forget and get a tongue-lashing from Emma,' Alexander groaned.

'Anything.' Benjamin sat forward looking intrigued.

'Do you know of a Lord Phillips, possibly fifty years or more?'

Benjamin took a moment to think. 'I cannot recall the name, but I can ask around someone is bound to have made his acquaintance. Why do you ask? Does he have a fancy for your sister?'

'God, no.' The duke looked around to ensure no one could overhear what he was about to say. 'Emma received a troubling letter from Lady Rebecca Rutherford this afternoon informing her of the brother's intention to marry her off to this Phillips fellow. My sister is expecting me to make enquiries this evening.'

'Ahhh, I remember your sister. Talked a lot, refused to brush her hair, she must have been a child of ten years old?' Benjamin smiled.

'She has not long turned twenty and is as troublesome as she was then, although she has a maid to brush her hair these days.'

Alexander laughed as they discussed his rebellious sibling. Both men were now laughing at the memory of the disobedient child with tangled hair who followed them around, prodding Benjamin with sticks when he didn't listen to her. It was hard to believe that the same child was now a grown woman.

Alexander was now in his carriage headed for home, Benjamin had agreed to ask around regarding Lord Phillips and promised to call on him when he had any information. It was a short carriage ride back to his townhouse and he looked forward to going to bed. Tomorrow, Lady Rebecca was to call, and he couldn't help but smile at the thought of what might pass between them.

CHAPTER SEVEN

Although the hour was late, Rebecca could not sleep. She lay in her bed staring up at the ceiling, wondering how many more nights it would be before she was gazing at another ceiling in a completely different bed chamber. The thought of sleeping in Lord Phillips's bed made her shudder, his mere presence had made her feel uneasy; she almost had to reach for the chamber pot as a wave of sickness came over her at the very thought.

Rebecca had no one to fight for her, both parents dead and sisters that were probably as keen as Robert to marry her off.

What must I do? I need to get away.

Hours passed and Rebecca had continued to toss and turn for most of the night, eventually drifting into a light sleep. Aware that Flora was now in the room, she sat up, the bedclothes quite dishevelled from her restlessness, her hair no longer in the neat braid that she had tied the evening before.

'Good morning my lady, did you sleep well?' Flora said softly.

Rebecca was not going to answer that. She feared if she answered, she would burst into tears, and that would not do at all.

'Would you be able to prepare a bath for me, Flora? I would also like to wash my hair. If the water could be a little cooler than my usual bath, I am rather warm this morning.'

Rebecca wanted to distract herself from the thoughts that were torturing her. She tried to appear cheerful as she got out of bed and having a cool bath might help relieve her of the tiredness she felt from her lack of sleep.

As Flora continued to make herself useful while the bath was being prepared, folding, and tidying anything in her midst, she studied Rebecca's demeanour, suspecting that something was amiss.

'His Lordship was very much in his cups again last night. There was broken glass all over the study floor John the footman has been sweeping it up this morning. Seems like the Earl dropped a full bottle of brandy on the Axminster. It doesn't half smell like an old tavern in there. Lily is on her knees scrubbing the carpets as I speak.'

Rebecca smiled when Flora mentioned the room smelling like a tavern.

'There it is, that beautiful smile, you do not seem to be yourself this morning, is everything well?'

The kindness of Flora's words was too much, Rebecca could not hold back her tears any longer. Clutching the damp handkerchief that was in the palm of her hand, Rebecca quietly shared her plight with the maid. She could see the look of pity in her eyes as she spoke of her brother's treatment and the way Lord Phillips had made her skin crawl.

'They are not kind men, Flora. I know I should not say it of my own flesh and blood, but I find my brother hard to love. There are times when I hate him.'

Rebecca felt a little better now she had confided in Flora; she knew that none of what was spoken would be shared with the other servants.

'Now, let's get you in the bath before the water gets any cooler and you end up catching your death. It makes me cold just thinking about it'.

Wearing a pale-blue gown with her hair styled into a neat chignon Rebecca now felt ready to face the day. She had yet to break her fast but felt little appetite and did not wish to see her brother just yet. She would be leaving soon to make the short journey to Emma's home, hopeful that one of her friends would have a solution to her impending doom. She was also eager to see the Duke again.

Thankfully, the Earl had not yet surfaced from his chambers when the carriage was brought round to the front of the house, allowing Rebecca to leave without explanation, accompanied by Alice, a young maid from the household.

Alexander had risen much later than he had planned, he had lots of business to attend to and had hoped to catch a glimpse of the ravishing Lady Rebecca, but after overindulging in whisky the night before he had drifted into a deep slumber. With the time now nearing noon, he sat alone tucking into a plate of eggs and bacon while glancing at the daily news sheet, the silence interrupted by the sound of female voices coming from the hall.

'Is she here, has she arrived? I could not help but worry that her dreadful brother would keep her locked in her room until the day of the wedding'.

'I feared the same, Matilda'.

'We are not certain that Lord Rutherford wishes for Rebecca to marry the gentleman at all. He may not even wish to court her. They may not even suit.' Emma was the voice of reason, even though she did not believe any of the words she was saying.

Alexander listened to the conversation as it continued outside the door to the breakfasting room.

Of course, he would want her, only a fool would not want her.

'Rebecca, thank goodness, you came. We were terribly worried that your brother would not allow it after yesterday,' Felicity said as she embraced her friend.

'He was still in his chamber abed when I left. I did fear the same thing. I suppose I should be thankful he was extremely drunk last evening and is likely sleeping off the effects. He caused quite a scene while in his cups, I am told.'

Rebecca repeated the story of the broken glass and the room smelling like a tavern while she removed her bonnet.

Alexander had witnessed the behaviour of the Earl and worried that he might do something to harm Rebecca if she were ever to defy his orders. He did not know the man, but he did not like him one bit.

The ladies were still gathered in the hallway when Alexander had finished his late breakfast, all of them franticly talking at the same time. Young ladies of the ton would not normally be so unbothered about what the etiquette was when visiting friends; removing their outdoor clothing, it became evident that they had their own rules when together. Alexander could not help but feel a certain respect for them, but also a sadness at what the future held, especially the thought of a woman such as Rebecca having to curtail her vibrant spirit for the sake of another. Alexander felt guilt as he recalled the conversation he had not long shared with his mother.

Do I care too much how others perceive me?

He did not want to become another gentleman of the ton who chose a young lady to marry solely to birth their heir, allowing the continuation of some precious title, keeping another outwith the marital bed as his whore for his sexual gratification.

Alexander had spoken with his sister earlier, informing her that a friend was hoping to obtain information from various acquaintances on who the mysterious Lord Phillips was. Now, seeing Rebecca in his home surrounded by her friends he was unable to comprehend how a brother could be so cruel and uncaring to their sister.

His eyes never left Rebecca, as he stood in the hallway, clearing his throat to make the ladies aware of his presence. So engaged in conversation, that they had not noticed him wanting to pass.

49

Rebecca looked up, Alexander had noticed that her eyes were puffy and bloodshot, but he still thought she was the most beautiful woman he had ever seen. Whether she was aware of the action or not, he was transfixed watching as she innocently ran her tongue along her lower lip before nibbling the corner. Not able to stand the temptation any longer and the possibility he would be caught staring, he offered the ladies a courteous greeting, politely bowing before making his way along the hallway. Curtseys were exchanged, along with the normal pleasantries afforded to a Duke, before Emma led her friends to the drawing room where they would take tea and discuss ways to help Rebecca.

The duke had not yet reached his study when he heard the sound of light footsteps at his back, turning around Rebecca stood barely an arm's length from him. They stood looking directly into each other's eyes for a brief moment before one of them spoke.

'Lady Rebecca, can I be of assistance?' he watched her carefully, unsure as to why she had followed him.

'Your Grace, I just wanted to say ...' She looked around, checking they were alone.

For the first time in her life, Rebecca found herself to be utterly at a loss for words. She was so mad with herself at that moment because she had planned on saying something improper just to irk him. It was becoming one of her favourite pastimes. Now she could not even say her own name.

'You wish to say what?' Alexander stood with his hands behind his back eager to hear what she had to say. She was now looking at the floor, shuffling her feet.

'Rebecca, there you are. Come, we have much to discuss.' Emma was beckoning to her from the doorway, wondering where her friend had gotten to.

Rebecca was thankful for her friend's interruption. She could not possibly be in the duke's company a minute longer and wondered if she would even manage a *good day*. With a devilish grin forming on her lips, she did something that she thought would nettle him, something she could still do since losing her power of speech. She cheekily winked at him as she had done in the park; the difference was, this time he winked back.

'What were you two talking about and why are you blushing?' Emma sounded suspicious as she linked arms with her friend whilst they walked back along the hall.

'You know how I like to torment his grace,' touching her cheeks with the palm of her hands Rebecca tried not to look sheepish as she felt the heat radiating from her face.

'Did he say something inappropriate? Should I tell him off? He has obviously said something. Why else would you be at a loss for words?' Emma enquired.

'Nothing untoward was said, I promise. Now, we have much to discuss.' Rebecca quickly changing the subject, and they continued to make their way to join the others.

As they were now all gathered together in the room, Felicity was the first to break the silence, none of the ladies having spoken for several minutes, which was highly irregular.

Each of them was trying to come up with a solution to Rebecca's unwanted betrothal.

'The ball. We need to come up with a plan for the ball,' Felicity announced.

The ladies sat up a little straighter interested to know what Felicity would say next.

'Do you suppose we could add arsenic to his drink without discovery?' Rebecca suggested.

'Lady Rebecca Rutherford, have you been bribing that nice young footman to acquire copies of the Penny Dreadful again?' Emma spoke as if she was scandalised.

Felicity put her teacup down, her face lighting up at the mention of the literary publication. 'Please say you have a copy! I have heard the servants speak of it ... Stories of vampires and highwaymen.'

'Felicity, I do not know why you have such an obsession with highwaymen. They are murderous scoundrels,' her cousin remarked.

Felicity answered Katherine by pretending to swoon. This caused the mood in the room to lighten as they chuckled at Felicity's dramatics. The ladies continued to discuss various ways that they could end Lord Phillips, deciding it was probably not a good idea to tie him to the rear of a runaway horse before the conversation once again turned serious. It was agreed that they needed to know more about the Earl before forming a proper plan that could be put into practice. Rebecca had a bad feeling in her stomach at the mere mention of his name, wanting to remain cautious; also, as an acquaintance of her brother, he was likely involved in all kinds of nefarious behaviours.

The ball was in two days and all the ladies in the room would be in attendance, as would Rebecca's three siblings.

'Can you not feign illness, Rebecca, and miss the ball altogether?' Matilda asked.

'If only it were that simple. Robert would never allow that. I could be abed with scarlet fever and he would still insist I attend.'

Her friends did not know whether to laugh or cry.

'I suppose I should consider myself quite fortunate to have a brother like Alexander, although he can be quite intolerable at times he only wishes the best for me,' Emma said.

Rebecca nodded at the mention of the word *intolerable* when Emma described her brother. It also gave her the opportunity to ask whether he would be attending the ball without raising any suspicion that she was becoming quite smitten with the young duke.

CHAPTER EIGHT

As he sat working at his desk, Alexander was still quite curious as to what Lady Rebecca had been about to say before his sister's interruption. She had looked extremely pretty yet vulnerable this afternoon, with the signs she had been crying. If they had been alone, he would have taken her in his arms and comforted her until she forgot her woes. Where he had first felt protective noticing the dark shadows beneath her puffy eyes, his thoughts soon turned to lust as she had openly nibbled at her lip, the sight of her pink tongue causing ungentlemanly thoughts. Then she had winked at him as they stood face to face outside his study, and he could not stop himself from playing her at her own game by winking back.

He should not have enjoyed her embarrassment so much; her blushes were a lovely thing to witness. As the duke contemplated how far her blushes might travel down her body, he was disturbed by Simpson. Simpson was a man who had been a loyal butler to the Fane family for many years and a great strength to the Dowager Duchess in her time of grief.

'Your Grace, Viscount Turner has arrived. Shall I send him in?' the butler announced.

It was not normal for the butler to assume that the duke would receive a visitor that had not been expected, but Alexander had mentioned that the Viscount may call during the week. Simpson had known Benjamin since childhood.

The tall, confident gentleman entered the room, with his usual lopsided grin. Alexander began pouring two large glasses of whisky, before handing one to the Viscount, motioning for him to sit.

'Nothing changes with your choice of spirits, my friend, always the hard stuff.' Benjamin winced as he took a sniff of the drink.

'You forget my mother is Scottish and if I drank anything other than her countrymen's tipple, I would be disowned instantly ... Although sometimes that does not seem such a bad idea when spoken aloud.'

Both men laughed before Alexander raised his usual toast. 'Slainte Mhaath ... Again, I do not know if I pronounce this correctly as a simple Englishman ... Slan-cha-va my friend. Good Health.'

'Nothing much changes with you either, Turner. I could ask my valet to give you a good haircut. Your curls are as unruly as they were when you were a lad.'

'And why in God's name would I want to do that, when the ladies adore them so much?' Running his fingers through his hair, Benjamin took another swig of his drink.

'Talking of ladies, I assume you are here as you have gathered some information on this Phillips fellow?'

'I have indeed. Sadly, it does not bode well for Miss Rutherford.' Benjamin took a sip of his drink as he shook his head.

Any joviality Alexander had been feeling during their current conversation or the memory of his earlier encounter with Rebecca had instantly evaporated at the thought of what he was about to hear next.

'It appears that Rutherford owes Phillips five thousand pounds in gambling debts.'

'How does that involve Lady Rebecca?' Alexander asked.

'Rutherford does not have the funds; he has all but gambled away the family home,' Benjamin replied.

'And?' the duke was starting to become impatient with the Viscount.

'The hand of Lady Rebecca Rutherford is all the Earl of Fordew has to offer, and it seems Phillips practically bit his hand off at the deal, desperate to be initiated within the ton and a betrothal to the sister of an Earl is the perfect opportunity,' Benjamin revealed.

'The *bastard!* His own flesh and blood', Alexander hissed. 'I will need to tell Emma, although she really should not get herself involved, but I doubt she will be able to help herself.' Alexander gave his word that he would inform his sister of any news and he never broke a promise.

Emma had been walking back along the hall after bidding farewell to her guests when she heard her name mentioned. The door to her brother's study was slightly open, so she breezed through it without knocking.

The two men stood when she entered. Paying no attention to whoever else was currently in the room, Emma headed straight over to her brother. Placing her palms flat on the hard surface of his desk, she leaned over in an ungainly fashion. 'I could not fail to hear my name mentioned, Alex. Do you have news concerning Rebecca's brute of a brother?' She could not disguise the anger in her voice as she spoke of him.

'Kindly mind your speech and calm down for a moment, Emma. Have you failed to notice that I have company?' the duke motioned over her shoulder with his hand, horrified at her sudden entrance.

Benjamin had certainly not failed to notice the delight that was the wriggling backside directly in his eyeline. When she turned, he found her front as delightful, if not more so, than the back view. Emma had turned to face him, half perched on the edge of her brother's desk, eyeing the Viscount curiously as if she recognised him but did not know how.

'You must remember my good friend, Viscount Benjamin Turner? You spent a large part of your childhood poking him with sticks.'

She kept her eyes focused on him, his handsome face looking directly back at her.

'Please sit, my lord. I am not one for all the pomp and ceremony required of us, much to my brother's frustration.'

Benjamin was quite taken aback at how the annoying, scruffy little child he had known had blossomed into such a Goddess. She had taken his breath away the moment she turned to face him, not in the slightest bit embarrassed or shy as she considered him. It took a few more minutes before realisation hit. Throwing her head back, revealing a slender neck, laughing while clapping her hands together in delight, Benjamin Turner could only imagine how it would feel to run his tongue down that beautiful neck.

'Of course, I remember you, Benji Turner,' Emma smiled, still sitting on the edge of the desk.

'Benjamin or Ben, if you please, my lady. I detest the name, Benji. Only you ever called me that!' the Viscount sounded quite irritated now.

'I do not think either is appropriate now you are no longer a child, Rebecca. It is rather familiar for an unmarried lady such as yourself,' Alexander scolded.

Alexander had tried hard not to laugh at the interaction, remembering how incensed the shortening of his name had made him; perhaps he would call him Benji, too if only to annoy him. Especially when the Viscount was being too pompous.

'Still the same arrogant countenance by the looks of things,' Emma replied to the Viscount.

'Emma Fane. Do not speak to the Viscount in such a way. It is inappropriate, even for you. I apologise on behalf of my unruly sister, Turner.'

'Do not worry yourself, Fane. The lady is correct in her assumption,' he scoffed.

'There was a time, my lord, that I fancied myself in love with you. What a silly child I was, with you *twice* my age.' Holding her belly as she laughed, Emma spoke as if the very idea of fancying Benjamin was ludicrous.

Although quite pleased with the idea she had once harboured an affection for him, even if it was childhood infatuation, he was also slightly crestfallen at the way she laughed at the notion of such feelings. Trying to keep up his rakish persona without being too flirtatious in the company of the duke, Benjamin found he enjoyed her teasing.

'I would hope you are not so foolish as to entertain such notions now, my lady,' he replied with a raise of an eyebrow.

'As a lady of twenty, I am aware there are certain types of gentlemen of which to avoid. I would suspect *you* are one of those gentlemen.' She said this in such a playful manner that Benjamin could not help but grin.

Feeling slightly wounded at her depiction of him, he still could not help being roused by her. She had a look of her brother due to similar colouring, but there was something about her eyes. It was not the colour, but the shape that entranced him: a perfect almond, framed by perfect black brows the colour of her hair. He snapped out of his musings when she rolled those same eyes at him before turning all her attention back to her brother.

Her eyes may be beautiful, but they are also full of obstinance.

'What do you have to tell me, brother? What do you know?' Emma had turned to her brother to ask the question.

'I think you should sit down,' Alexander nodded his head to the chaise.

Sitting down, she listened intently as Alexander and Benjamin told her what they now knew. Occasionally shaking her head or releasing a small gasp, she remained silent. When there was nothing left to say on the matter, Emma stood. A single word had still not crossed her lips before she excused herself from the room, heading upstairs to her private quarters.

CHAPTER NINE

It was the day of the ball and Rebecca was lying on her back once again staring at the ceiling of her room. Contemplating.
I could run away, become a governess, work in a tavern even ... that might be fun.

Her sisters had arrived and had been speaking with Robert downstairs. As she lay fully clothed on the counterpane there was a knock on her door. Before she could even say *enter,* Rosalind glided in with Flora at her back looking very much the Viscountess she was. Rosalind was an attractive woman, as were all three sisters, but in more of an aristocratic way than Rebecca. Her posture was perfect, and her gowns were always of the highest quality.

'Rebecca, what on earth are you doing? You have a ball to prepare for,' her sister spoke as she looked around the room.

'I feel the beginnings of a headache. I wish to rest some more,' Rebecca complained.

Her sister was not fooled by her sibling's words and carried on as if she had not spoken at all.

'Flora, organise a bath for Lady Rebecca while I decide on which gown she should wear,' the viscountess said as she looked at Rebecca with irritation.

Maybe if I wore a coal sack, he would refuse me?

'Rebecca Rutherford, will you stop wool-gathering and pull yourself together? tonight is a very important evening for us all,' Rosalind snapped as she proceeded to search through her younger sister's gowns.

'And why is that sister?' Rebecca knew exactly what Rosalind meant.

The Viscountess seemed a little flustered, choosing to ignore her younger sibling, holding up a green gown. 'Perfect. This is the one.'

The dress that her sister had decided upon was one of the more risqué in her collection, with a neckline much lower than her other gowns. The garment was quite beautiful, and she was more than happy to wear it, but she knew it was for the benefit of the loathsome Lord Phillips. The modiste had convinced her to try a more alluring style when she had turned one and twenty and this was the result, although yet to wear it as it was so unlike anything she had worn before. She had never contemplated that its debut would be an occasion as awful as she was sure tonight was going to be.

~

The journey to the Strathdee residence was conducted in silence. Sitting opposite her in the carriage, her brother did not converse with her once. Not criticising or bullying her for the duration of the journey, she knew he must be satisfied with her appearance this evening. Rebecca could not decide if this was a good thing or a bad thing. It was all very unnerving.

Eventually arriving after what felt like an age, Rebecca smoothed down her skirts, straightened her gloves and took a deep breath. When exiting the carriage, Robert offered her his arm, presenting himself as the doting elder brother when they entered the mansion. The opulent entrance and hallway were lined with candles that brightened up the darker spaces, illuminating the floor-to-ceiling mirrors, the soft lighting flattering to a person's countenance. The strong fragrance of the fresh flowers that adorned every surface was so potent Rebecca felt her nose twitch. She had barely handed over her shawl before her brother grabbed her by the wrist, forcefully dragging her into a secluded corner that was not visible to the other guests who were continuing to arrive.

As the Earl put more pressure on her wrist, she tried not to make a sound, fearing what he might do, noting the coldness in his eyes as he turned to face her. The smell of stale alcohol and tobacco radiated from every one of his pores. Lifting his free hand to point a finger in her face, Robert looked around to check they were alone before he spoke.

'Tonight, you will be the perfect Lady. When you see Lord Phillips, you will be attentive and agreeable, and you will keep that shut.' He pointed his finger at her mouth after barking his orders.

All Rebecca could do was nod in agreement while rubbing her wrist to stop the stinging, relieved when he had released her from his grasp.

'Now take my arm and put a smile on that bloody miserable face,' he snarled.

Alexander had been awaiting Lady Rebecca Rutherford's arrival. When she had entered the grand ballroom on her brother's arm with her fake smile, he could sense her sadness. She looked incredible in the pale green gown that enhanced her perfect shape, accentuating her small waist, loose tendrils of chestnut hair hung against her creamy skin drawing attention to the upper swell of her breasts. Alexander fidgeted with his signet ring while trying to stay composed as he observed every rake and libertine in the room eyeing her lustfully as she crossed the floor.

Rebecca looked around the room for her friends, hoping to escape her brother's watchful eye. It did not take long before she saw Matilda beckoning her from a nearby corner where she stood with her other friends. The Earl of Fordew was now conversing with a few gentlemen that he was acquainted with, briefly introducing her. The men each looked at her for a second before quickly dismissing her and carrying on talking as if she was not there, which had given her the opportunity she needed.

Rebecca apologised demurely for interrupting the conversation before asking her brother's permission to be excused so she could speak with Lady Matilda Brookfield, knowing it was unlikely that he would refuse her while in the company of others. The daughter of a duke, Matilda Brookfield was ranked higher than the Earl, so refusing his sister's request would cause much gossip and speculation within the ton.

Alexander continued to watch the woman that had begun to invade his thoughts day and night; the thoughts at night being the most enjoyable. Lady Rebecca had now escaped the clutches of her brother and was walking across the floor towards her group of friends. Taking a sip from the drink he held tightly in his hand, the duke's eyes never left her as he watched carefully while she interacted with his sister and her other confidantes.

'Fane'. Benjamin Turner approached holding a glass of champagne. 'You are looking very serious this evening. Does Lady Rutherford know what her treacherous brother has been up to yet?'

Benjamin had followed his friend's gaze to the corner of the ballroom where a group of pretty young ladies were huddled together with serious expressions. The two men were taller than most men of the ton so were able to see much of what was taking place from where they were standing. 'I think she is just about to find out,' Alexander replied.

'Ahhhhh ... There they stand, the most alluring, beautiful ladies in attendance,' Benjamin spoke while gazing towards the five friends.

Alexander looked at his friend quizzically.

'Did you know that most of the single gentlemen here, and some married of course, desire at least one of those ladies but are quite intimidated by them when they gather in their little group? It is all rather amusing to watch.' the Viscount spoke before taking a large swig of champagne.

Benjamin had not paid much attention to them in the past as he preferred cavorting with more experienced ladies. But now he was desiring one of the ladies himself which he would never admit to his good friend who was also the lady's brother.

'How so?' Alexander was curious at the Viscount's comment.

'You will notice that when one Lady becomes separated from the group, she will be practically pounced upon by a Lord desperate to mark her dance card. Your sister included.'

'Each one of them is quite outstanding in their own way. They are often the talk of the games room. I would never have imagined that one of the ladies would be your annoying little sister', Benjamin sniggered while sweeping his hair off his forehead, before letting it flop rakishly back down again.

'Do not be having any lewd thoughts about Emma, Turner. You are nothing but a rogue when you see a pretty face,' Alexander threatened jokily.

Or Lady Rebecca for that matter!

'As if a man would be intimidated by a group of young innocents.' The duke laughed, wondering if he had been slightly intimidated by Lady Rebecca when they had first met. Her beauty took his breath away while her behaviour incensed him.

Taking a glass from a passing footman, drinking it then taking another from the silver tray, Alexander continued to watch the scene unfold as Rebecca shook her head and threw her hands up to her face while her friends looked at her with despondency.

Rebecca felt as if she was in a very bad dream as she learned from her friends that she had been offered to Lord Phillips in return for writing off her brother's gambling debts. She knew her brother was cruel, but this was worse than anything she thought him capable of.

'How could he do such a thing? I will never allow it. There must be something I can do. I cannot marry him, I simply cannot.'

'We will do all we can to prevent this, I will speak to Papa. Maybe he can help?' Matilda offered. Her father was a powerful man and well respected in the ton.

The other ladies nodded their heads, hopeful that Lady Brookfield's father would forbid the marriage once he knew of the circumstances surrounding it, although it was unlikely that a duke would intervene in something considered another family's business, no matter how deplorable.

'I think I need to take some air; will you excuse me?'

Rebecca needed to process what she had just been told. Although she loved her friends dearly, the noise of their chatter, along with their sympathetic looks, was doing nothing to calm her heart that was beating so fast she feared it might beat right out of her chest at any moment.

'One of us shall come with you,' Felicity said, her gloved hand taking hold of Rebecca's.

Shaking her head, Rebecca informed her friend that she would rather be alone for a while as she considered what she might do. The revelation had been quite a shock, but she promised that she would come straight back before walking away.

Rebecca did not know whether she should have stayed on the balcony in view of the other guests or be more daring and walk alone in the garden. It was beginning to get dark and would be easy for a lecherous Lord to haul her into a secluded part of the grounds.

Maybe I should allow myself to be compromised by another, then he might refuse me.

Being found in a compromising position would certainly ruin her for any decent marriage. An idea that may have horrified her previously now did not seem so awful. It seemed like a better alternative than what was about to befall her.

As Rebecca wiped away a solitary tear, she flinched at the pain from her wrist which she had forgotten until now. Removing her glove, she was taken aback by the red imprints left from the pressure of her brothers' fingertips. Fresh bruising was now becoming visible on her lower arm. She wanted nothing more than to scream so everyone could hear; it was not a scream due to the physical pain but one of anger, wishing she could tell the world what a bullying brute her brother really was.

Pacing back and forth trying to make sense of everything she had just been told, she was suddenly aware of the sound of footsteps approaching. Panicking that her brother or Lord Phillips had followed her outside, she lifted the hems of her skirts and ran behind a large oak tree, covering her mouth with her gloved hand so that her heavy breathing wouldn't alert them to her presence.

Alexander had watched Rebecca leave the ballroom alone. If he had seen her, he feared others would too, including Phillips who was currently talking with Robert Rutherford while salaciously eyeing the youngest debutantes.

The man really was a repugnant bastard.

Alexander was overcome with that same protectiveness he had felt before. She was not safe outside, on her own, in the dark. He had hoped that he would not startle her, but she had run off at the sound of his approach, and now hiding behind a tree; although not very well as he could see as well as hear the rustling of her skirts.

She is so lovely and endearing.

If not for the current circumstances, he might have laughed at her terrible attempt at concealment, but he knew that she was likely afraid at this particular moment. It would be better to tread carefully.

'Lady Rebecca. It is only me, the Duke of Sandison.' He loathed using his title, but it would not be proper for an unmarried lady to be familiar with his given name.

'Your Grace,' she whispered.

Alexander smiled at how adorable she looked, peeking around the huge tree. Her eyes wide with relief, her gloved hand frozen over her mouth.

'You need to improve your hiding skills,' he smiled.

'I feared you were someone else, your grace. I had little time to consider my hiding options!' She answered more abruptly than she had meant as her heart was still beating franticly.

'Is it Phillips or Rutherford that you fear?' He knew it was but wanted to hear it from the lady herself.

'I do not fear them, your grace. I *loathe* them. They disgust me.' Another single tear ran down her cheek, landing on the grass at her feet.

Alexander could not stop himself from stepping closer, close enough to smell the sweet floral scent that radiated from her. Noticing that she wore only one glove, her other hand bare, she rubbed the gloveless wrist in a soothing motion while flinching slightly.

'Is there a problem with your wrist Lady Rebecca? Does it pain you?' he enquired sympathetically.

'A little, but not so much,' she replied softly.

Rebecca followed his gaze as he gently took her small hand in his, lifting it so he could get a better look, the moon now being the only source of light. When he had stopped examining her wrist and arm his eyes met hers once more.

'Who did this? Was it Rutherford?' Although filled with rage, he spoke as gently as he could as he did not want to frighten her.

'I promise you; it is fine your grace. Please do not concern yourself.'

The duke could not bring himself to release her hand, relishing the feel of her soft skin against his gloveless fingers. Rebecca began to feel a fluttering in her lower belly as Alexander gently held her hand, the skin on his fingers felt rougher than she had assumed it would be; it had the feel of a man who was not afraid of manual work. She liked it; most men of his rank would object to any form of hard work preferring to do nothing at all. Rebecca took an intake of breath when she felt his thumb casually stroke her wrist, ensuring it would not cause her any pain. As they looked at each other, neither uttering a word, the only sound they could hear was the light wind that blew between the trees mingled with their breathing. Without releasing eye contact Alexander raised her wrist to his lips and kissed it softly, her pulse beating franticly at his touch. Before she knew it, she was in his arms his hands on her waist pulling her tightly to his solid form. Rebecca let out a squeal in surprise as she was imprisoned against his firm chest.

'Your Grace, what are you doing?' she said breathlessly.

'Do you recall the last time we were alone Rebecca?' he teased.

The intimacy of her name on his lips made her heart quicken. His hands gently squeezed her waist.

'Do you recall what you said to me Rebecca, *mmmm*?' he asked while stroking her lower back. She nodded shyly. 'What did you say to me, lovely Rebecca?'

There was a slight pause as she looked into his piercing blue eyes, surprised by his words.

'You think me lovely, your Grace. I am sure you think me a lot of things, but I would never have considered *lovely* to be one. Possibly vexing, irritating … even maddening.' Rebecca was nervous as he held her close, starting to chatter endlessly.

'That does not answer the question. Let me remind you,' he whispered in her ear, leaning in closer.

Even though she was overcome with desire as his large hands now caressed her back, she refused to allow him the satisfaction of repeating the words she had spoken in the library. She was going to be the brazen woman that he assumed her to be. Nervously sliding her hands up his chest until they rested on his shoulders, the feel of his arousal twitching against her, his breath quickened when she turned her head slightly. She allowed her mouth to brush his cheek, delighting in the feel of his stubble, trying to sound composed although she had never felt so nervous.

'A person can change their mind, your Grace, can they not?'

Before he could consider her words, Rebecca was standing on her tiptoes, placing a gentle kiss on his lips. That was the only prompting he needed before passionately covering her mouth with his own, guiding her until her back was against the oak tree: the same tree that he had caught her hiding behind minutes earlier.

Alexander had not followed her into the garden with the intention of ravishing her, but as she stood before him looking positively breathtaking in the moonlight, he *had* to touch her. When she had placed her soft lips against his, he had to have her. As she welcomed his kiss, Alexander hungrily ran his tongue along her full mouth, coaxing her lips apart, allowing his tongue to merge with hers. Rebecca instinctively did as he did, their tongues touching, the kissing becoming more frantic. Rebecca grasped his hair, inciting a groan from him, his hand moving down to fondle her backside. She could feel her nipples hardening beneath her bodice, her breasts suddenly feeling heavier. His hands moved from her bottom, stroking her sides before moving up to her aching breasts. Rebecca gasped into his mouth before pulling away from the kiss as his thumb stroked and pinched her hardened nipple through the silkiness of her dress. He repeated the caress on the other nipple while he watched her, her mouth open revealing the tooth gap he loved, her cheeks flushed with desire. His hands still on her breasts, he ran his tongue over the shell of her ear before gently nipping the lobe.

'Your Grace, we must stop …this is madness,' Rebecca panted.

'Do you wish me to stop Rebecca, just say the word and I will walk away?' his lips did not leave her neck as he spoke.

'No, I do not … it feels wonderful, but I am sure it is wrong and if anyone caught us ...'

Alexander smiled against her skin while she talked; he had noticed earlier she prattled a lot when nervous.

Continuing to trail kisses down her neck, he slid the sleeve of her gown down to reveal a bare shoulder. When he felt her body shiver, he stopped to look at her, the taste of her skin fresh on his lips.

'I will ask you again, my darling. Do you wish me to stop?' His voice was low and husky.

Breathless, all Rebecca could do was mouth the word *no* and he was kissing her again, groaning into her mouth. Her body pressed against his growing manhood; she could feel the wetness at her core.

Overcome with feelings of desire, she tentatively ran a hand down his front so she could feel the hardness of his chest before her hands travelled under his jacket, resting on his back delighting in the warmth of his body radiating through his finely cut waistcoat. Alexander made a growling noise as her hands gently explored his body, almost losing control and spending in his trousers as she hesitatingly touched his backside. He had never been so aroused. If she had been a woman of experience, he would have lifted her skirts and thrust himself into her wet cunny until she screamed his name, not caring if his bare arse was visible in the moonlight as he pounded into her.

Lightly nipping her bottom lip with his teeth, he repeated her name, kissing along her jawline, licking down her neck until his tongue reached the upper swell of her breasts. Alexander impatiently grabbed at the fabric of her gown, his hand moving under the material, desperate to touch her bare skin.

'Say my name, Rebecca ... Call me Alexander.'

'Alexander, I need more. Please,' she pleaded.

Rebecca rested her head back against the tree, watching the hunger in Alexander as he devoured her body with his mouth, his warm hand was now beneath her gown, travelling nearer to where she wanted it most. Groaning in pleasure, just as his finger grazed the damp area between her thighs, Rebecca suddenly gasped when out of nowhere she noticed a bright light that seemed to be getting closer to where they were, along with the faint sound of feminine voices.

'Alexander!' she whispered.

The duke was so immersed in the ravishing of Lady Rebecca Rutherford that he was unaware that they were about to be caught devouring one another against a tree, until Rebecca forcefully pushed him in the chest.

'Someone is approaching, your Grace' she fretted, standing up straight.

As the voices grew closer, Rebecca recognised one of them as Emma's. Her friends must have been worried and were now outside searching for her. Rebecca had no idea how long she had been gone from the ballroom.

'I cannot be seen with you like this.' Her voice was pleading with him to do something.

Reaching out, Alexander cradled her face with his large hands, kissing her hard on the lips before quickly disappearing into the darkness like a character from one of her favourite novels. The only trace of him was the faint smell of lavender on her skin. Gathering herself, rearranging her gown and patting down her hair, she took a deep breath.

'Emma, is that you?' Rebecca called out in the darkness.

Seconds later, she saw her four friends appear by candlelight. Katherine was the first one to throw her arms around Rebecca. 'We have been so worried about you Rebecca, you have been gone so long.'

'I am sorry I did not realise. Time just ran away with me, I had much to consider. Is my brother looking for me?' Rebecca asked.

'Not that we know off. I suspect he is still in the card room. My brother saw him earlier,' Emma answered.

Rebecca was glad for the darkness when Emma mentioned the duke as recalling what they had been doing minutes before, she felt her face redden.

What would he be doing to me now if we had not been disturbed?

'I believe that your sister, the Viscountess, was looking for you just now. I told her you were in the retiring room; she thinks I am going to fetch you,' Emma announced.

'Thank you, Emma. I suppose I should return now.' Rebecca hooked arms with her friend as they slowly walked back to the ballroom.

Alexander stood alone in the darkness allowing a reasonable amount of time to pass before making his way back to the ballroom. He would much rather have jumped in his carriage and returned to his townhouse after what had transpired between himself and Rebecca, fearing he would not be able to take his eyes off her, desperate to take her in his arms again. The last thing he wanted was to rouse suspicion amongst other guests. Standing in the moonlight with his hands resting flat against the tree where he had found Rebecca hiding, he contemplated what he had done.

Although annoyed at his lack of self-control he did not regret touching her soft skin, still sensing the feel of her lips against his. His fingertips had barely touched her naked thigh as he stroked a hardened nipple through her gown, but he was more aroused than he had ever been. Alexander had seduced and bedded many women on his tour, but none had affected him in the way Rebecca had.

It was a good thing they had been interrupted because he was not sure if he could have resisted stripping off her dress to taste every part of her delicious body. She was so responsive to his touch; the sound of her heavy breathing alone was enough to make him spend in his trousers. Shaking his head, he idly picked at some tree bark while waiting for the time to pass, before snapping back to reality.

What have I done? I am a scoundrel; I took advantage in her time of need.

Rebecca and her friends had re-entered the crowded ballroom, the Viscountess spotting her instantly, now heading in her direction with a scowl on her face.

'Where have you been sister, we have been searching for you?' she snipped.

'I needed some fresh air; I have a terrible headache, Rosalind,' Rebecca replied while placing a gloved hand to her temple.

Rebecca was not paying any attention to her sister as she chastised her, her mind being elsewhere as she looked around to see whether Alexander had returned to the ballroom.

'Now, will you put a smile on your face dear and stand up straighter as Lord Phillips is on his way over? He will expect a dance,' Rosalind fussed.

Rebecca felt her heart sink, she had just had the most enjoyable experience of her life just moments earlier, but now she was to share a dance with a man that made her skin crawl. The feeling of Alexander's hands on her would soon become a distant memory as they were replaced by the lecherous touch of Lord Phillips.

Alexander had discreetly returned and was now standing at the far end of the ballroom with Benjamin at his side when his sister Emma joined them.

'Brother, you are frowning more than usual, are you not having a good night?' Emma knew her brother hated functions such as this.

'Tedious sister, it is all so tedious,' he replied, rolling his eyes.

'And you Benji ... have any married ladies caught your eye this evening?' Emma teased.

Both men opened their mouths in shock at her comment; it was not expected that young ladies knew of such a thing. Alexander looked around, grateful that no one had overheard his sister's comment. Benjamin had a furious look on his face, far too speechless to offer a quick retort, as she looked at him innocently. Her comment was quickly forgotten when the duke spoke through gritted teeth.

'Phillips.'

The three of them watched from a distance as the detestable lord greeted Rebecca with a kiss to her knuckles before leading her to the dancefloor. It was even more unfortunate that it was a waltz which was a much more intimate dance.

Alexander did not think he could bear to watch another man with his hands on her waist, the same waist that he had caressed earlier. He watched the interaction for a few minutes before it became too much. Not wanting to cause a scene, he swallowed what was left of his drink, laying down his empty glass, excused himself, and then left.

Rebecca tried not to flinch as Lord Phillips placed his sweaty hand on her back as he led her to the dancefloor, his eyes fixated on her breasts rather than her face. She had always been self-conscious of her breasts as they were larger than what was considered fashionable and often tried to hide them with the dresses she wore. Phillips did not even try to disguise his lustful gaze which was making Rebecca very uncomfortable. So uncomfortable, she had to stop herself from fleeing the floor.

'You are looking very beautiful this evening my lady', he said, his hand inappropriately squeezing her waist.

'Thank you, my Lord,', Rebecca squirmed. If he did that again, she might just stomp on his foot.

As the music began, they glided over the floor with the lord not saying much as his eyes swept the busy ballroom. Rebecca had not failed to notice how he watched the much younger ladies of the ton, unable to hide the lecherous look on his face.

The dance had felt like the longest dance of her life. Phillips was so close to her she could smell his breath, which was a mix of alcohol and whatever fish dish he had eaten for dinner. Rebecca tried to find something likeable about the man, although it was becoming incredibly difficult the more time she spent in his company, getting to know his true character. The dance eventually ended; with the Lord escorting Rebecca back to where her sister Rosalind stood with a satisfied look on her face.

'Thank you for the dance, my Lord.' Rebecca was delighted that the dance was over so genuinely sounded happy when she spoke.

Kissing her knuckles a little longer than was considered appropriate, Phillips announced that he would call on her the following morning at *eleven o'clock sharp*. Before Rebecca had a chance to object, he then bowed before walking purposefully into the crowd. Taken aback at the Lord's parting words, Rebecca turned to face Rosalind with a look of horror.

No no no no no.

'Excellent, all is going to plan, dear sister. You shall be betrothed very soon.' Rosalind clasped her hands together in delight, not caring about her sister's distress.

'I do not want to be betrothed to him, Rosalind. He is a *disgusting* man. Please do not make me,' Rebecca complained.

'We will not discuss this in public, Rebecca. Robert and I shall speak with you at breakfast tomorrow.'

Rosalind was soon distracted when her husband, the Viscount, appeared at her side. Rebecca thought how unfair it was that her sisters had been allowed to marry for love, while she was being forced to marry a man that she despised.

Emma had been watching the events as they unfolded alongside Benjamin; the two of them had not spoken to each other since Alexander had left.

'I truly thank you for the stimulating conversation, Viscount but must bid you farewell now, as my friend looks as if she needs me,' Emma said in a sarcastic tone.

'Do not let me stop you, my lady. Your company has been most pleasant. Off you trot now.' Benjamin tried to keep a smirk from forming, knowing that his words would rile Emma.

'You are so, so, so ...' Emma was almost stamping her feet in frustration at his rudeness.

'Handsome ... charming,' he said while flashing perfect white teeth.

'Maddening, utterly maddening, as you always have been... *Benji*'

Spinning on her heels, Emma could not stand being in his company any longer. She could hear his conceited laugh as he mumbled something about her still being in love with him, which she most certainly was not as she stormed off.

Rebecca was once again surrounded by her closest friends. Emma was the last to join them, her face flushed as she was still shaking with anger.

'Whatever is the matter, Emma?' Katherine asked. 'You look like you wish to kill someone.'

'Do not tempt me, Katherine. Benjamin Turner must be the most aggravating, vain, conceited gentleman I have ever met.'

'Is that the gentleman who was with the duke earlier?' Felicity asked.

'Yes, I have known him since I was a young girl but have only just re-encountered him these last weeks. He has been helping my brother gather information regarding Rebecca's brother and Lord Phillips.'

'He is deliciously handsome, Emma. Are you sure you do not hold some affection for him?' Felicity gave Emma one of her cheeky smiles and a wink causing her cheeks to redden at the assumption.

The other ladies giggled at the look of horror on Emma's face before remembering the real reason they had gathered in the corner where they could not be overheard.

'Rebecca, you must tell us everything that has happened this evening so we can plan our revenge,' Felicity once again spoke as if it was a plot from a novel.

'Oh, it is all so awful. Lord Phillips is to call on me tomorrow morning. My brother and sister wish to discuss my betrothal over breakfast before he arrives. It seems that my fate is sealed, I have no choice in the matter now. When we danced, I could not bear the feeling of his fat clammy hands on me. I felt positively sick when he leered at my breasts. How am I to share my life with such a brute? I would rather die.' Rebecca could feel tears welling in her eyes.

'Oh, my dear, dear friend. We shall not allow this marriage to happen, we *promise* you. Tomorrow, after Lord Phillips has paid his visit, we must gather together and end this debacle once and for all. You shall *not* pay for your brother's failures.' Lady Emma Fane had never sounded more determined.

The friends accepted Emma's invitation to take tea with her the following day, praying that Rebecca would not be forced into an unwanted engagement with the Lord anytime soon.

CHAPTER TEN

Alexander was breaking his fast the following morning in one of the worst moods he had been in for as long as he could remember, when his mother and sister joined him. They sat close to him, making it easier to converse with each other rather than shouting from the other end of the long table.

'Good morning, mother. Good morning, Emma.' He was not in the mood for conversation but refused to appear rude.

'Good morning, my darling boy. What irks you so this morning?' The dowager duchess instantly recognised when one of her beloved children were not themselves.

'You did leave the ball in an awful hurry Alexander. When I returned several hours later there was light coming from your study. Did something happen?' Emma sounded concerned but also spoke as if she knew what was bothering him.

'Just not in the mood,' he grunted, returning to reading the news sheet.

Emma and her mother gave each other a knowing look. They would not try and converse with him when he was in such a foul mood.

'So, Emma. Did you enjoy the ball?' her mother enquired as she buttered a slice of warm bread.

'I have had more enjoyable evenings. I am so terribly worried for Rebecca, mama. Her brother and sister want to talk with her this morning before Lord Phillips calls. She fears he is going to propose marriage.' Emma wiped a tear before it ran down her cheek. 'I feel so hopeless as I have no idea how I can help her.'

'Poor, poor girl. She is so beautiful and full of life. She deserves to marry for love. You are very fortunate that you will never be forced into an arranged marriage like so many young ladies of the ton, Emma. Is that not so Alexander?'

Alexander snorted from behind the paper he held aloft, obscuring his face. He had not read anything since they had mentioned Rebecca's name, listening intently to the conversation.

'What was that noise for brother? Do you plan on offering me to a wayward lord, just to be rid of me?' Emma asked the moody duke.

71

Alexander folded the news sheet before placing it on the table. He lifted his cup and sipped his now lukewarm coffee. 'If you are not married by the age of four and twenty, I may have to give that idea some serious thought, sister,' he replied.

Alexander was desperate to ask Emma what had unfolded at the ball after Rebecca had danced with Phillips but did not want to seem overly interested in her friend.

'Alexander, can you help in any way? You are a duke, after all?' Emma asked.

'How can *I* help; I do not know Robert Rutherford or Lord Phillips. I barely know Lady Rebecca Rutherford.' Alexander thought that he was beginning to know the lady quite well.

'You could do some more investigating. You learned of the gambling debt, did you not?' Emma reminded him.

'It is Viscount Turner that you have to thank for that Emma. He has more associates in London than I do.'

'Can you speak with the Viscount again? I would speak with him myself, but he is so exasperating I can barely be in the same room as him without getting cross,' Emma complained.

'I do not know what you expect us to do, Emma. We cannot tell her brother what he can and cannot do when it concerns his sister,' Alexander said.

Alexander would love to give Rutherford a damn good pummelling for the way he treated Rebecca. If he discovered he was hurting her physically, he would kill the bastard. But she was not his to protect.

Why do I feel so protective over her? She is not mine.

Alexander was eager to leave the room before he revealed something in his facial expressions that might divulge how he felt about the whole situation; whether this was his deep hatred for the earl or his growing feelings toward Lady Rebecca.

'I have much work to do, ladies. I will be in my study for most of the day. Emma I will speak with Benjamin this evening at my club'.

Walking around the table, he kissed his mother gently on the cheek before making his way to the door.

~

Rebecca had another restless sleep after what had happened the night before, her recollection of the excitement she felt when she was in the duke's arms replaced by the loathing she felt for Phillips. How the touch of his hands on her could make her body react so differently to how she felt when the duke had touched her.

Dressed in a pale pink gown with her hair tied loosely at the nape of her neck, Rebecca looked at herself in the mirror. She gave her body a shake and took a long breath before heading downstairs to join her siblings for breakfast. When Rebecca entered the breakfasting room, all three of her siblings were already seated at the table. They had obviously been there for some time as they had all finished eating and were now conversing while drinking tea, quietly enough so the servants could not listen in.

'Decided to join us, Rebecca?' Stating this, Robert preferred to look at the older sisters as if they should be impressed by his snide comment.

Rebecca refused to answer him as whatever her response was it would likely escalate into a full-blown argument, and she did not have the energy for that. Her two sisters did not even offer a greeting when she joined them; they had glanced at her briefly before looking away. If she was not mistaken Rebecca, thought her sisters appeared slightly sheepish. Robert, on the other hand, had his usual arrogant, entitled smirk on his face.

'We have much to discuss Rebecca, and I do not have all day. I am a busy man', the earl said coldly.

'I am here now, Robert, so you might as well get it over with. You expect me to marry the odious Lord Phillips because you cannot repay a gambling debt,' she exclaimed.

Rebecca had surprised herself with the sudden outburst; her words were out before she had time to consider the consequences. Both sisters gasped and flinched when Robert slammed his fists on the table, sending crockery flying. Pieces of cutlery cascaded to the floor. When a young footman instinctively stooped to clear up the mess, the earl shouted at him and the other servants to get out. Charging around the table, Robert came up behind Rebecca, leaning over her so he could place his hands on the arms of the chair where she sat.

Roughly pulling her chair from the table while Rebecca remained seated, he hauled her around until she was facing him, staring into her panicked face. Determined not to show any weakness, she returned his intent look, clasping her hands on her lap.

'Robert. Please calm yourself.' Rose was the first of the sisters to speak. 'I am sure Rebecca is sorry for what she said.'

'I am *not* sorry, for it is the truth, Rose,' Rebecca said.

Robert's hands were now on Rebecca's slender shoulders, squeezing as he shook her. 'No sister of mine will speak to me in such a way! There are times when I can hardly believe we are of the same blood.'

That is one thing we can agree on then.

'I only speak the truth, brother. Your recklessness has finally caught up with you and I am the one who must suffer.' Rebecca refused to look weak in front of him, fixing the earl squarely in the eye.

The next moment, Robert removed his hand from her shoulder, raising it as if to slap her but was quickly stopped by Rose's pleading. Seconds later, Rebecca hastily jumped out of the chair as her brother stepped aside before escaping the room.

Rebecca had fled to her bedchamber, fearing she had pushed her brother too far, thankful that he had not followed her and punished her with his bare hands. Lying on the bed, her face buried in a pillow that was now damp from her tears, she was lost in her turbulent thoughts when there was a light knock on the door.

'Rebecca dear. It is Rose. Can I come in?'

'Please go away Rose. I want to be on my own.'

Although she had asked her sister to leave her alone, the door to her room slowly opened, Rose entering cautiously. Heavy with child, Rose made her way to the armchair nearest the bed, letting out a heavy sigh as she lowered herself to sit.

Rose smiled. 'Are you going to talk to me, Rebecca? I do not plan on having this child in your bedchamber.'

Rebecca sat herself up on the bed, feeling guilty that her heavily pregnant sister had become involved in this whole scenario when she should be at home resting.

'Does your husband not worry that you are out when you are so close to the baby being born, Rose?'

'This is our third child, my dear. I have assured him that I will know when the time is near,' Rose replied, resting her hands on her swollen belly.

'You are so lucky that you married for love,' Rebecca sighed.

'I am so very sorry for what has happened. It seems that Robert has no choice and will lose everything if this marriage does not go ahead, Rebecca.'

'But it is so very unfair Rose. Is there nothing you can do to help? You must see that Lord Phillips is an awful man. I *cannot* marry him.'

'Sadly, as women we do not always have a choice in such matters. I am so very thankful that my darling husband allows me the freedoms many ladies of our social standing will never have,' Rose said.

'I know we have never been particularly close, but do you really wish to see me live a life of misery with a man I cannot stand to be around? I am not naive to what happens between a husband and wife in the bedchamber Rose. I cannot face it, please, I *cannot*.'

It was at this point that the tears began to flow freely again. Rebecca noted that her sister's eyes glistened with her own unshed tears as she listened to her plight. Perhaps her sister did care for her after all.

~

When Lord Phillips arrived, Rebecca was taking some air in the garden. Standing with her back to the house that she had lived in her entire life, gazing into the distance, Rebecca thought of the earlier conversation with Rose. It was the first time she had ever felt any kind of compassion or sympathy from one of her siblings. Approaching footsteps interrupted her musings; turning around, she saw a maid approaching.

'My Lady. His lordship requests your presence in his study.' The maid curtseyed before scurrying off, a sympathetic look in the young woman's eyes. Servants were known to gossip, and she had likely heard the many conversations revolving around Rebecca's impending betrothal.

Walking back to the house, Rebecca noticed her sister, Rose standing at an upstairs window. When their eyes met, her sister dipped her head before disappearing from view.

Robert was standing facing the open door to his study. Because he was taller than the man he was conversing with, he was able to see Rebecca over his guest's shoulder. An arrogant smirk on his face, Robert watched her entering the room, pausing his conversation before moving aside and raising his arms to beckon her in.

'Ah sister. Did you enjoy your morning stroll around the gardens?' he asked.

Rebecca pinched her lips together to stop herself from commenting on the insincerity of her brother's words. 'I did, thank you. It is a fine morning.'

Lord Phillips was studying Rebecca, his eyes flitting between her breasts and her face. A line of sweat sat on his top lip that he patted dry with a crumpled handkerchief. When he proceeded to use the same handkerchief to blow his nose, the action almost made her retch.

'Lady Rebecca. May I say how delightful you look this morning. Perfectly radiant,' Phillips said.

Graciously bowing to the Earl, she accepted the compliment, aware that her brother was observing every interaction with a warning look.

Signalling for them to sit before taking a seat behind his desk, Rebecca noticed that her brother had a half-empty glass of spirits sitting alongside the papers and ledgers littering the old desk that had been in the Rutherford family for generations. It was obvious that he had been drinking due to the slight stagger when he walked.

'Now, sister, as you are aware, his Lordship has asked me for your hand in marriage, and I have given him my blessing,' the earl casually announced.

Lord Phillips grinned before crossing his legs and leaning further back into the plush armchair. Rebecca did not look up, afraid that she would burst into tears or scream, so she just nodded resigned to her fate.

'It will be a small wedding, and your sister Rosalind has agreed to do all the planning required. We will procure a licence and hopefully schedule the date for approximately four weeks' time,' Robert declared, swirling the amber liquid around in the glass that he held, before throwing his head back and swallowing the contents greedily.

'Oh, that is awfully soon, my Lord. Surely, we should get to know each other a little better. What if we do not suit?' Rebecca was aware that she should have agreed without hesitation so as not to incur her brother's wrath, but she could not stop herself from speaking.

'And why do you think we would *not* suit, my dear?' the lord asked, amused at her words.

Before she had the chance to reply, Robert stood up, moving around his desk so he now stood leaning over her. Rebecca looked at her brother's face, drawn to the small thread veins that were visible on his red and puffy cheeks. His eyes were tinged yellow.

'It is done. His Lordship is happy with the match, so nothing more is to be said. You are now excused, Rebecca. Rosalind awaits you in the parlour.'

Both men were now on their feet as Rebecca stood to leave. All she could do was pleadingly look at her brother while he waved his hands in a shooing motion towards the door.

~

Rosalind and Rose were both sitting in the parlour, they had been chatting to each other but stopped when their youngest sister walked in. Rose stood and Rebecca did something she had never done; she threw herself into her sister's arms, allowing the tears to flow.

'Now, now my dear, everything will be fine, come sit with us,' Rose murmured, allowing her sister the embrace, stroking her back in soothing motions.

Rebecca sat herself down, taking a sip of cold tea as she took time to compose herself. Her throat was quite sore with all the crying she had done recently. Rosalind tried offering her a handkerchief, but she refused, preferring to use her own. As far as Rebecca was concerned, Rosalind was as much to blame for this as her brother.

'How can you agree with this, Rosalind?' Rebecca had stopped crying, her sadness now turning to anger.

'It is a good match for you Rebecca. Lord Phillips is a very wealthy man. You will live a very comfortable life,' Rosalind replied.

Rebecca rested her elbows on her knees as she held her head in her hands. 'I do not care about his wealth. I hate him. He is loathsome.'

'Rebecca Rutherford, you should be grateful that he will have you. It is about time you started to behave like a lady. You are becoming an embarrassment to the family name with some of your recent behaviour. This marriage will surely be the making of you,' Rosalind said.

Rebecca could see that her sister was finding it difficult to control her temper but as usual, she remained the perfect Viscountess. Calm and unemotional.

Rebecca could not stay in the room any longer, feeling claustrophobic with the beginnings of a headache. 'I cannot talk of this any longer, sisters. Please excuse me.'

Rebecca looked at Rose who had her hands resting on her large belly, mouthing what looked like the word *sorry* while Rosalind insisted that they would speak later.

~

Half an hour later, Rebecca's carriage pulled up outside Emma's house. Accompanied by a maid that she had bribed with some coin to chaperone, she had told her sisters she was going for a walk rather than telling them the truth due to the possibility that her brother would hear and forbid Rebecca from visiting her friends.

Alexander was returning from an errand when he saw Lady Rebecca alight from the carriage outside his residence. On seeing her, he felt the urge to shout her name and run to her. She was talking with her maid as she ascended the front steps, his long strides allowing him to catch up with her just as she knocked on the front door. He cleared his throat to make her aware of his presence rather than speaking, allowing himself a moment to catch his breath so it was not obvious he had rushed to meet her.

Rebecca jumped slightly at his sudden appearance. 'Oh, your Grace. You startled me.'

Even though she had a wide smile, Alexander noticed that her eyes once again showed signs that she had been crying. When she opened her mouth, he struggled to divert his eyes away from the tooth gap he found so appealing, wishing he could pull her into his arms and cover that beautiful mouth with his own and run his tongue over those perfect teeth.

The butler had opened the door and was waiting patiently for his master and Rebecca to enter, trying to divert his eyes as the two of them stood on the steps looking at each other in silence.

The awkward moment was broken when Emma magically appeared from behind the butler, looking relieved, if not anxious. 'Rebecca, you managed to come. I am so pleased; we were so worried'. Barely acknowledging her brother as he entered at the same time, she chattered to Rebecca while he handed his hat and gloves to a footman.

Emma was suddenly distracted by a passing maid, allowing Alexander the opportunity to move close enough to Rebecca so he could whisper in her ear, speaking softly so his sister would not hear. 'We need to speak. Come to my study if you can ... *alone.*'

Rebecca felt the familiar fluttering in her lower belly as their fingers touched, desperate for him to kiss her the way he had in the garden. Nodding her head and smiling, she left him standing on his own as she followed Emma along the hall.

~

The friends were gathered in the library as they had done many times before, although this was a much more sombre meeting. They each embraced Rebecca when they saw her, the kindness shown causing more tears to flow.

'We must not allow this marriage to go ahead. We have some weeks to plan but I assure you, we will not let it happen,' Emma said.

'Even if we must steal you away, Rebecca,' Katherine replied.

'We have made a pact.' Felicity and Matilda giggled as they both spoke at the same time.

Rebecca sat up straighter on the small sofa, interested to know about this pact, already feeling better about the whole situation.

Further down the hallway, Alexander stood looking out of the window, trying to take his mind off the fact that Lady Rebecca Rutherford was currently in his home, frustrated that he could not touch or flirt with her, hoping that she would come to him as he had requested. He had initially wanted to apologise for what had happened between them on the night of the ball, having convinced himself that it was only a passing infatuation. But now all he wanted to do was take her in his arms again.

He had never met a woman like Rebecca. Obviously beautiful, she also possessed an air of confidence that made her seem fearless. Alexander had also witnessed a vulnerability that made him want to protect her. The reaction from his body when they had kissed was unlike any feelings he had felt before. Alexander had never been intimate with an innocent, surprised at how responsive and willing Rebecca had been to his touch. It only made him hungry for more, but he was not going to take her innocence from her; that would be reserved for her future husband. But the mere idea that her husband-to-be was the repellent Phillips made him want to punch a fist through the windowpane, now knowing that the man had a reputation for heavy drinking, gambling, and seducing *very* young ladies.

Just as Alexander was about to pour himself a much-needed whisky to calm his temper, there was a light knock on the door. It creaked open to reveal a vision of loveliness dressed in pale pink.

'Can I enter, your Grace? I do not have much time before my friends will wonder where I am.' Rebecca sashayed into the study, peering around at the unfamiliar surroundings.

Taking long strides towards her, Alexander quickly closed the door before anyone noticed her coming in. He knew she was unusually nervous as her delicate hands shook slightly as she held them at her front. Already, he could smell the sweet scent of her perfume in the room. They just looked at each other for a moment as if neither of them knew what to say; it was Rebecca who moved closer to the duke and spoke first.

'You wished to speak with me, your Grace? I am imagining that you wanted to tell me how sorry you are, and how much you regret what happened between us in the garden?' She paused waiting for him to speak. He remained silent.

'Have you lost your voice, your Grace? I do not care if you regret what happened between the two of us because I do not. It was the most exciting and passionate moment of my life; I am about to be married to a man that I loathe and am unlikely to ever experience passion like that ever again.'

There she is chattering away because she is nervous, she is so adorable.

Alexander thought it quite amusing that she would not stop talking, so decided to let her carry on for a little longer.

'My brother advised me this morning that I am to wed Lord Phillips in four weeks' time. If my future is to be with a man who repulses me, a man whose touch makes me nauseous whenever I think of it, I want to be seduced and ruined by someone that I desire first, to experience passion and ...'

I have to stop her now or she may never stop talking.

'Rebecca, please be quiet for a moment,' his voice was laced with amusement. 'I was not going to say any of those things you mentioned.'

'Oh.' Rebecca looked slightly embarrassed, her cheeks turning pink.

'I have not been able to stop thinking about you Rebecca. One moment you drive me to utter madness and the next I want to ravish you until you scream my name.' Alexander knew that he should not talk to an innocent young lady in such a way, but the expression on her face made it worthwhile.

Before he knew what was happening, Rebecca had moved forward and thrown her arms around his neck. Grabbing her by the waist, desire taking over, he pulled her body closer. Desperate for her to feel how hard she made him, his lips and tongue trailed down her slender neck as she panted his name. Rebecca was equally aroused, grabbing his hair with one hand while her other tentatively moved lower, curious to touch the hard bulge that pressed against her belly.

'Oh God, Rebecca. If you touch me like that again, I will take your innocence right here in this very room,' he groaned.

They continued to kiss each other, their hands urgently exploring each other's bodies over their clothes, neither caring that they were standing in the middle of his study and could be caught at any moment. The thought of someone walking in on them sent a thrill through Rebecca.

Pulling apart to catch a breath, Alexander reached out and cupped Rebecca's cheek before running his thumb along her lower lip, drinking in her beauty for a moment before he leaned in to kiss her again. Just as their lips touched again, there was a knock on the door.

'Bloody Hell! Why do we keep getting disturbed?' His frustration prompting ungentlemanly language in front of a lady, Alexander rested his forehead against Rebecca's, both breathing heavily, still aroused. Rebecca giggled into his shoulder at his outburst, not unfamiliar with him using words which she heard frequently at home.

'One moment', the duke shouted, recognising the knock as that of his butler, allowing them a moment to compose themselves.

'Should I hide?' Rebecca asked, reluctantly removing herself from his embrace.

'Probably be a good idea,' he smiled.

Looking around, she decided to slip behind the heavy velvet curtains where she could remain hidden from view. Kissing Alexander on the cheek, Rebecca scurried over to the window before the butler was given permission to enter the room and then announced that Viscount Turner had arrived. Luckily, he was waiting in another room which meant

Rebecca could flee the study undetected after the duke left to receive his visitor.

~

'What have you been doing, Rebecca? We thought you had gone home,' Emma smiled when her friend returned.

'Was I gone for such a long time, Emma?'

'I met your brother and Viscount Turner in the hallway, and we had a brief conversation about Lord Phillips.' Although she hated lying to her closest friends, it had been the perfect excuse to explain why she was gone longer than anticipated. She could not very well admit that she had been frolicking with a duke right under their noses; and one of their brothers at that!

Now Rebecca was back with her friends, the conversation returned to her impending marriage. It was decided that Matilda would be the one to inform Rebecca of what they had already discussed.

'We are all aware of how horrid your brother can be, Rebecca. We know that you do not speak of it, but we have seen the marks on your skin and the contempt in his eyes when you are with him.' Matilda blinked back tears as she spoke.

Rebecca lowered her head as she listened to her friend's words.

'It is difficult to hear one speak unkindly of family, but you do not need to suffer this alone, Rebecca. We are going to help you. We will end all of this,' Matilda continued.

Rebecca was willing herself not to cry when she answered, 'How I would love to believe you, truly I would, but I cannot think of a way out of this.'

Matilda looked over to Emma, signalling that she should now say her piece. 'Rebecca, we worry that your brother might harm you again if you do not comply with his wishes.' Emma lifted a package from the floor handing it to Rebecca.

'What is this? I hope it is not an early wedding gift, that would be most inappropriate,' Rebecca said.

'REBECCA RUTHERFORD, how can you say that?' Emma cried. 'Katherine has a maid that is of similar size to you. For some coin, the woman agreed to sell some of her clothing. A dress, shawl, bonnet, stockings and boots. She has also made a promise to Katherine that she will never speak of it, or she will lose her position.'

Rebecca looked a little confused.

'The clothing is for *you* Rebecca, if you need to escape your brother. No one should recognise you, giving you time to get away. We have all read about similar plots and they *always* work', Felicity said.

'But. But where would I go?' Rebecca asked.

'You come straight here. This is the closest place to your home. You *run* if you must. It matters not if it is the morning or the middle of the night,' Emma said sincerely.

'Do you really think that I should fear my brother so much?'

'Yes, we do Rebecca. Until he has you married to Lord Phillips, he is capable of *anything* to keep you from running.' Felicity answered, the other friends nodding in agreement.

Considering everything that had been said, Rebecca ran her hand over the package. She had suffered her brother's rage for most of her life but had never known her friends felt the way they did. 'What if Robert sees me return with the parcel?'

Emma left the room, returning a short time later with a large hat box, taking the parcel from Rebecca, placing it inside and securely replacing the lid.

When Rebecca took the giant hat box home, her brother was not about so she went straight up to her chambers unchallenged. Removing the package from the box, she unwrapped it before hiding the bits amongst her clothing. Rebecca would tell Flora but no one else.

~

Alexander, Emma, and the dowager Duchess rarely sat down to dinner together; this evening was different as Alexander had hoped to hear more of Rebecca's upcoming nuptials.

'It is not often that you dine with us, my darling.' The dowager said as she looked at her son warily.

'Do not be so suspicious, mother. I have spent far too much time alone in my study lately. I desire some company and conversation that is all. I may even go to my club this evening', Alexander said.

'I think it is wonderful that you are dining with us, brother'.

The three of them had always enjoyed each other's company, chatting and laughing as they recalled stories of growing up, sharing fond memories of the late Duke. Alexander did not want to ask Rebecca, hoping his sister would update their mother on the most recent events during the conversation, aware that his mother was very fond of the young lady. He did not have to wait much longer before the dowager enquired after her.

'Did Lady Rebecca visit with the other young ladies today dear?' she asked.

'Yes, I am still incredibly worried for her, Mama. Her brother is so vile to her and is forcing her to wed in a matter of weeks,' Emma exclaimed.

The dowager Duchess put down her wine glass, shaking her head. 'It is quite the mystery as to how such a sweet girl can be the sister of such a deplorable young man. She was always treated differently from the others. Rebecca was only a bairn of five years when her mother died.' Evelyn said.

'She does not speak much of her life growing up, Mama. Was it so awful for her?' Emma asked.

Alexander looked at his mother, keen to know more of the woman who had captivated him.

'Her father never recovered from the death of his beloved Mary. It was always rumoured that he saw too much of a resemblance to his wife in Rebecca, finding it painful to even look at her. The poor child never knew what affection or love was. Her father passed when she was but one and seven, her brother becoming the new earl at the age of two and twenty. He was irresponsible and unlikeable even then, a wicked bully.' The dowager tutted and shook her head as she talked to her children.

'She has had such a terrible life, Mama. We cannot allow her to spend the rest of it in a loveless marriage with a man she despises,' Emma snivelled.

'What do you think you can do to help, Emma? You must not interfere. As much as you care for your friend, her brother is responsible for her.' Alexander would love to have offered his sister a solution, but he had none.

'Brother, you know that he does not care for her. And you also know the reasons for the hasty betrothal. It is all so unfair. Can you not offer him a loan to pay his debts?' Emma asked.

'Emma, you cannot say such a thing to your brother. It is not his responsibility,' the dowager scolded.

'You know that I would do anything for you, sister. But the debt is five thousand pounds and that is an awful lot of money.'

'My dowry. I will offer *my* dowry,' Emma replied.

'I am sorry, but I will not allow that.' Alexander was torn. He was developing feelings for Rebecca Rutherford, but he was not willing to hand over such a large sum of money to a man who would surely use it for means other than paying his current debts.

~

As her brother was entertaining some unsavoury associates at home, Rebecca had taken her evening meal in her chambers. Earlier, when she had been returning to her room from the library, a soused gentleman she had never seen before tried to block her path. She had feared that he would have lunged for her if he hadn't been disturbed by a passing footman, giving her the opportunity to push past him, run to her room and lock the door behind her.

It was not unusual for Robert to entertain at home. Rebecca had hidden in the darkness once before out of curiosity, witnessing half-dressed women and drunken revellers running through the halls, unfamiliar sounds coming from behind the closed doors.

Rebecca heard a gentle knock on the door, signalling that Flora had come to aid her in getting ready for bed. Nervous that it might not be her trusted maid, she cautiously opened the door, feeling unsafe in her own home. If she felt unsafe now, what was it to be like when she was married to a man she knew nothing of?

'Quick, Flora. Close the door and turn the key,' she said in a panicked voice.

'Why, whatever is the matter my lady?' Flora had never seen Rebecca behave in such a way.

Rebecca relayed the story of the man in the hallway as she paced the floor.

'That is dreadful, my Lady. You must tell his lordship of it,' Flora said.

'He would not care, Flora. He dislikes me so much; he would likely encourage it.'

Flora decided to stay with Rebecca for far longer than she normally would in the night-time. They sat up gossiping about the other servants and various members of the ton until they both began yawning, signalling to them that the hour had become very late. As soon as Flora left, Rebecca locked the door to her room, so shaken by what had happened earlier she used all her strength to drag a chair across the floor to wedge against the door.

~

The following morning, Rebecca sat alone at breakfast, grateful for the silence. The events of last night had made her consider whether she felt safe in her own home and what her future might be married to someone who was so well acquainted with her brother. She wondered if Lord Phillips was amongst the revellers last night, partaking in the drinking, gambling, and sexual pleasures offered to him. The very thought of it made Rebecca quickly lose her appetite, so she decided to return to her bedchamber.

When she got to her room the door was open, which seemed strange; she was always careful to close it, as were the servants of the household when doing chores. On entering, she was greeted by the sight of her brother rifling through her private possessions.

'What are you doing?! How dare you enter my private chambers?' Rebecca yelled a little too loudly, alerting the earl to her presence.

When he turned to face her, she was quite startled by his countenance. Robert had always been considered a handsome man. Now, standing before her, his bloodshot eyes glaring, his face puffy and red, he had the appearance of a man twice his age. 'Where is the jewellery?' he growled.

Rebecca was puzzled at his question. 'What jewellery?' she asked.

'Do not act bloody stupid, girl. The jewellery that mother left you. I know there was a sapphire brooch. Where the hell is it?' he snarled, continuing to rummage through her belongings.

Rebecca knew exactly where the brooch was but there was no way she was going to tell him, so she kept up the pretence. 'I promise you, brother, I do not have any of mother's belongings. Maybe you are mistaken. Is it possible that Rosalind or Rose have it in their possession?'

His eyes practically bulging out of his head, she had never seen him look so angry. 'I do *not* believe you. And *this*. What is this?' he roared, holding one of her gothic novels above his head.

'That is mine. Give it to me, Robert,' she cried, trying to grab it back but failing.

'Have I not already forbidden you from reading these vile books? Why do you have to disobey me at every turn? Do you take pleasure in it?'

While she continued trying to grab it from his grasp, Robert began ripping pages from the book, the shreds fluttering to the floor. 'You will *not* leave this room until you tell me where the brooch is. I know you are lying to me, Rebecca.' He stood so close now she could smell the stale alcohol on his breath, spittle spraying from his mouth the angrier he became.

Before she had the chance to react, he had taken the key, slamming the door behind him, and locking her in. Rebecca fell to her knees, tears streaming down her face as she collected the torn pages scattered on the rug.

CHAPTER ELEVEN

It had been three days since Emma, Katherine, Matilda, and Felicity had heard from Rebecca and they were becoming extremely concerned.

'I think we should call upon her this afternoon,' Felicity said, articulating what all of them had been thinking. Although it was not normally the done thing to call on a person without prior notice, Emma immediately called for a carriage to be brought round.

Having been away on ducal business for a few days Alexander arrived home to hear the now familiar sound of female voices coming from the drawing room. After days spent negotiating deals and working long hours, he was glad to be home, and now the thought of seeing Rebecca after a long tiring journey instantly lifted his mood.

Straightening his jacket and smoothing down his hair, he impatiently entered the drawing room under the pretence that he was informing his sister of his return. The duke's eyes scoured the room looking for Lady Rebecca. Realising she was not there, he remained hopeful that she was in his home somewhere, reminding himself of the first time they had met. He knew he could not ask her whereabouts without his sister asking impertinent questions as to his interest in the young lady.

Emma turned to acknowledge Alexander when he stepped into the room, unable to hide the worry etched on her face. It was at that moment that he knew something must be wrong.

'Emma, is everything well? Has something happened while I was away?' he enquired.

The young ladies looked at each other before returning their gazes to Emma as if they were giving her permission to speak.

'We do not know anything for certain, Alexander. But we are most concerned for Lady Rebecca,' Emma said.

'What do you mean you are *concerned*?' Alexander felt a tightening in his chest at the words his sister had spoken.

'We have not heard anything from her in three whole days. It is so unlike her, brother. I have just called for a carriage to be readied so we can call on her right away.'

'She may be unwell, Emma, and may not want any visitors. Do you think it wise to just turn up on her doorstep unexpectedly?'

'Even if Rebecca is unwell, she would almost certainly send a note or message through her maid. Something is very wrong, Alexander. I am sure of it,' Emma replied.

'Do you think this has something to do with her impending marriage?' he asked.

'Most definitely. We discussed our concerns with Rebecca regarding her brother and his treatment of her. We have all seen the marks and bruises she tries to hide with her gowns and gloves.'

Alexander began to feel a sudden rage come over him, the thought of Robert Rutherford laying hands on *his* Rebecca made his blood boil. The duke had never thought of her as *his* before.

I must stop thinking of her in such a way. She could never be the perfect duchess I require. I could never wed her; she has not been brought up for such a duty.

He contemplated the possibility of taking her as his mistress if she was forced into a loveless marriage with a man she detested. Why would she not want to take a lover? By the way she had reacted to his touch, he was convinced that she desired him as he desired her.

~

The carriage arrived outside Rebecca's home just as a light rain had started to fall. Disembarking with the help of the young footman, the four young ladies hooked arms as they climbed the steps to the weather-worn front door. The large brass knocker in dire need of polishing now at eye level, Felicity boldly stepped forward and knocked twice.

Answering almost immediately, the butler was momentarily taken aback at seeing the young ladies that stood before him. Female callers to the Earl's residence would normally visit under the cover of darkness, wearing too much rouge and too little clothing; the polar opposite to the gently bred ladies that were currently standing on the front steps.

'May I help you?' he scowled.

'We have come to call on Lady Rebecca', Emma gave her best smile to the elderly man.

'I am afraid that Lady Rebecca is unable to accept visitors at this time,' the man informed them, taking a step back as if to close the door.

'And why is that?', Emma folded her arms in front of her, looking defiant.

'I am led to believe that she has caught a chill and has taken to her bed to aid her recovery,' he replied.

'Well, that is just ridiculous. Until today, the weather has been glorious.' Emma had now stepped closer to the po-faced man, looking him directly in the face.

His expression was unflinching. 'I am sorry my lady, but I really must bid you a good day,' he said before closing the door.

The ladies were now convinced Rebecca was being held against her will, likely because she had disobeyed her brother in some way. Walking along the pavement to where their carriage waited, Emma was aware of someone following them before she heard her name being called. Spinning around, Emma recognised that it was Flora, looking flustered and out of breath.

'Flora dear is everything alright', Emma said.

'I have been waiting around the corner for you, my Lady. I must be quick. Lady Rebecca gave me this, knowing that you would come.' Flora handed over a page that had been ripped from a book. Emma accepted the paper from the maid that she knew well, holding her hand for a moment.

'What has happened, Flora? Is Rebecca safe?'

'Lady Rebecca is quite well, but his lordship has forbidden her from leaving her chambers. I think the note will explain. No one can know that we have spoken my lady, or I shall lose my position', Flora said.

'Do not fear, Flora. We promise not to tell a soul. But if you need anything, you must not be afraid to call on one of us,' Emma spoke sincerely to Flora as she still held onto her hand.

'Lady Rebecca knew you would come; she is certain that you will help her. I must go now but please do what you can, my lady.'

Flora rushed off, leaving the ladies standing in the street, each with a look of concern for the maid who cared for Rebecca as much as they did.

Now settled in the moving carriage, Emma unfolded the paper that she had been given, recognising it as a page torn from one of Rebecca's favourite novels. The other ladies waited in anticipation as Emma began to read the words written in Rebecca's hand.

My brother has locked me in my chambers, forbidding me from leaving the house. I do not feel safe in my home anymore. I have faith in you all to save me.
R

The note was very short, evidently written in haste; scrawled over the top of the book's printed text, the handwriting had not been easy to decipher. Rebecca loved her books too much to tear a page from one and certainly would not deface it by writing over the words she valued so much unless desperate. They sat in silence for the remainder of the journey, each of them considering what they should do next.

Alexander sat at his desk, unable to concentrate on the ledgers before him. All he could think about was Rebecca. He had to stop himself from insisting he travelled to her home rather than his sister and her friends. It would have been both awkward and suspicious, as he would be unable to explain why he was so interested in Lady Rebecca's welfare.

The ladies had been gone for longer than Alexander had anticipated, the wait for their return was driving him mad. Realising he was not going to get any work done until he knew Rebecca was safe, he stood by the window, looking out to the street below, willing them to come back with news. He did not have long to wait before his sister's carriage approached; anxious to know the outcome of the visit, he left his study and made his way along the hall.

Emma had returned on her own, the other ladies having each gone home reeling from the words Rebecca had penned. When Alexander met his sister at the front door, he took one look at her face and felt a sense of panic.

Oh God, please let Rebecca be safe.

'Did you see her, Emma, was she home?' the duke questioned his sister as if his concern was for her rather than Rebecca.

The moment her brother spoke, Emma burst into tears, tears that she had managed to contain all the way home. Alexander placed a comforting hand on her arm, her body trembling as she cried. Opening her reticule, she handed him the note. Alexander hesitantly took the piece of paper from Emma's trembling fingers, scanning the missive, turning the ragged paper over in his hands while processing the words.

'I do not understand. Why would she rip a page from a book to write this note, Emma?' he said.

'I have no idea. But I do know that Rebecca would *never* destroy a book. Felicity thinks it must have been her brother. He forbids her from reading the books she loves; he once threw a collection of her favourites onto the fire. Rebecca would have wanted us to know how he is treating her. The earl is aware that it is the worst punishment he can bestow upon her. She cherishes her books. Her home is not a happy one, Alex. Reading is the one true pleasure that helps her forget,' Emma sobbed.

Alexander felt a lump form in his throat at his sister's words. 'The young lady always seems so happy and full of life?' he said.

'She is not unhappy, brother; she enjoys life, and we always have so much fun. But she does not know any different and cannot yearn for something she has never known. She is not as fortunate as us. Her family do not love each other as ours do.'

~

Later that evening, Alexander sat in the well-used armchair, broodingly swirling the amber liquid around the glass that he grasped in his hand. Barely aware of the other patrons in the room, he thought of Rebecca, alone and confined, not even a book for company.

'Fane, you were miles away. What troubles you, my good friend?' Benjamin sat down just as another glass was placed on the table between them, proceeding to pour himself a drink from the bottle that Alexander had procured on arrival. 'I suspect that it is a woman that invades your thoughts. I have seen many a gentleman with that look,' Turner mocked.

Alexander took a sip of his drink, a smirk forming at the corner of his mouth. 'As much as I would love to say that is not the case, I am afraid you are correct in your assumption,' he sighed.

'Ahhhh ... And who is the unlucky lady? Is she someone that I know ...? And does she have a friend?' Benjamin leaned forward, his elbows on his knees.

'It pains me to say but I am unable to get Lady Rebecca Rutherford out of my mind. She invades my thoughts day and night,' Alexander said.

Benjamin threw his head back and laughed so loudly that a few of the older gentlemen looked over at him in contempt. 'Well, well, well, your Grace. I did not expect *that*, although I *do* see the attraction. She is quite lovely', Benjamin chuckled before Alexander glared at him for using the word *lovely* when talking of Lady Rebecca.

'Does the lady know how you feel?' the Viscount asked.

Alexander quickly looked away, refilling his glass, hopeful that his friend would not see the guilty look on his face.

'Something has happened between the two of you. Please tell me you have not compromised the lady.'

'Bloody Hell, Ben of course not. But we may have shared a kiss ... Or two.'

Alexander took a large swig of whisky after his confession, surprised that he had spoken the words aloud. Benjamin ran his fingers through his unruly hair, more than a little shocked by the duke's proclamation. They had often discussed how they would never dally with innocents, no matter how alluring or tempting they were.

'It gets much worse, I am afraid.'

Alexander began to tell Benjamin about the note and what his sister had relayed to him earlier that day. Refilling their glasses several times during the conversation, Benjamin was as determined as Alexander to release Rebecca from her brother's evil clutches. Both men were now quite drunk after spending the last hour discussing possible solutions to Rebecca's predicament when they spied the very man they had been talking about.

Robert Rutherford strutted into the room, heading directly to the card tables, taking a seat, arrogantly snapping his fingers to summon for a drink to be brought over. Several inebriated gentlemen were conversing and laughing with the earl, patting each other on the back while throwing back more and more alcohol.

Benjamin and Alexander had been watching the interactions carefully for several minutes before giving each other a discreet nod. Standing, they casually made their way towards the table where Rutherford sat, each of them pulling up a chair. The other young lords sitting at the table already knew Viscount Turner, who proceeded to introduce the duke who noticed Rutherford eyeing them suspiciously.

'I do not recall us ever being introduced', Benjamin had turned to speak to the earl.

'Robert Rutherford, 3rd Earl of Fordew,' he spoke without looking up, an unopened pack of cards in his hand. The dismissive attitude from the earl when answering the Viscount instantly riled Alexander. The duke could easily have launched himself across the table and wrapped his hands around the arrogant bastard's throat.

How could he be related to someone as sweet and lovely as Rebecca?

'Are we going to play or are you all going to spend the evening nattering like daft chits?' Rutherford threw some coins on the table, before looking directly at Alexander.

Alexander ordered a fresh bottle of spirits to the table, pouring a glass for each of the gentlemen before the opening hand of cards was dealt. If the plan was to work, Alexander and Benjamin had to convince Rutherford that they were of similar character to him. Drinking copious amounts of alcohol and losing at cards was the easy part; being civil to the earl was far more demanding. Alexander had to excuse himself on more than one occasion, taking himself into another room until his temper cooled. The night continued to progress well as Rutherford began to relax in their company. Eventually, the hour was getting late and most of the club's patrons were leaving, but the earl was on a winning streak and was keen to carry on.

'It is time that I left before you take any more of my money, Rutherford', Alexander laughed as he continued to play the part of a carefree duke.

'I must agree with my good friend', Benjamin slapped the duke on his back, quite unsteady on his feet.

'We should do this again, in a more private setting, with higher stakes?' Rutherford slurred his words, one hand resting on the card table to steady himself. 'One day a week I invite a select few to my home. We play cards, drink fine wines, fuck beautiful women ... or men if that is your preference.'

Alexander may have been well and truly in his cups but that did not stop him from thinking of Rebecca and what she had to contend with at home.

'I will send details with the address and time ... and bring plenty of banknotes.' Laughing as he turned his back to them, Rutherford staggered towards the door, raising his arm to wave them farewell.

'Until next time', Alexander slurred before the two young men shook hands with the earl, nodded and left.

~

Rebecca paced her room unable to sleep, occasionally stopping at the window to admire the stars. She had opened the curtains, fantasising that the Duke of Sandison would arrive on horseback to steal her away. She had watched a carriage draw up in the darkness, a footman opening the door, revealing her very drunken brother as he fell to the ground. It took another three footmen to carry him indoors. All she could do was shake her head at what was not an unfamiliar occurrence.

Flora had managed to give Rebecca's hastily written note to Emma. All she had to do was bide her time in the hope that her friends were hatching a plan. Rebecca had chosen to write the note on the page her brother had torn from the book. She knew that it would be a clue to how Robert was treating her as she would never consider defacing any book. She had even been in two minds about whether to write on the page but knew that it was the logical thing to do. Her friends would know her plight was getting desperate.

CHAPTER TWELVE

Alexander sat in his study with a blinding headache. He would have regretted his overindulgence the night before if it had not been for the invitation that he weaved between his fingers. The Earl of Fordew's greed had played right into their hands.

When he and Benjamin had concocted the ruse, they had not expected it to be so easy. They had intentionally allowed the Earl to win each game of cards while leading him to believe that they were both hard-drinking, gambling degenerates. Men exactly like Rutherford was himself, which was why Alexander now held an invitation to his residence. The earl had invited the two friends under the illusion that he would trounce them both at cards while filling his pockets in the process. The last two days had felt like forever for Alexander as he had been quite desperate for the day to arrive when he would receive the invite, allowing him to put his plan into motion.

Benjamin sauntered into the room right on time, looking very much the wealthy gentleman that he was, with his expensive clothing and his usual air of entitlement. Looking up, Alexander reclined back in his chair, throwing the invitation on his desk when the Viscount entered.

Benjamin eyed the note, smiling as he read it. 'Well, my friend, are you looking forward to an evening of debauchery?' Benjamin flung himself onto the chair opposite the duke.

'You must not be distracted by lightskirts and good brandy. There is only one reason for tonight's ...'

'What is happening tonight, brother?' Emma had entered the room so quietly neither man had noticed; she waved her hand at them both to remain seated.

'Nothing for you to concern yourself with, sister.'

'Come now, Alex. I know when you are up to something. Tell me, what are you plotting.' Emma asked.

Alexander said nothing in response. He looked to Benjamin, hoping that he would offer up some witty remark that would change the course of the conversation, but his friend seemed to be too occupied watching Emma in a way that made Alexander both irritated and uncomfortable.

'What about you, Benji, will you tell me?' she goaded.

The look of longing on Benjamin's face quickly changed to that of annoyance at her teasing.

One day I will take her over my knee if she does not refrain from calling me that.

Alexander was not going to tell his sister of their plans; he loved Emma but knew that she would be unable to keep anything they told her regarding Rebecca secret from her friends, and the fewer people that knew the better. He also did not want her asking for details of the evening, which would likely be most inappropriate for a young lady such as herself.

'I think it is time we left. I will speak with you tomorrow, Emma. Good evening.' Alexander crossed the room and placed his hands on Emma's shoulders before physically turning her around to face the direction of the door. She tutted and gave both men a displeased look before marching out mumbling to herself.

'What was that?' Alexander looked at Benjamin with narrowed eyes.

'If I am not mistaken, that was your very irritating younger sister,' he replied.

'For a moment, I thought I saw you look at my sister in a very ungentlemanly manner.' Alexander frowned.

Benjamin stood, turning his back to the Duke so he could not read his face. 'Ha ha. You are very much mistaken, your Grace. The lady irritates me far too much to consider her romantically.'

"It is not thoughts of romance that concern me,' Alexander said, before calling on a footman to ready a carriage.

As the carriage pulled up outside the Earl of Fordew's residence, Alexander adjusted his cravat that already felt too tight around his neck. Seated opposite, Benjamin ran his fingers through his hair, making his appearance even more rakish than normal.

'So, Turner. We are in agreement as to how this evening will proceed?' Alexander was keen to get the evening over with as quickly as he could.

'Of course. We have gone over it several times now have we not. I will distract Rutherford with cards and brandy, letting him win initially. Do not worry yourself, Alexander, you will find her,' Benjamin said.

On entering the townhouse, Benjamin looked quite delighted when a scantily clad redhead brushed past him, offering a lascivious look as he eyed her ample breasts barely hidden beneath her low neckline.

'I do believe this evening may not be as bad as I had initially anticipated,' the young Viscount laughed as he rubbed his hands together in jest.

'We are here for a reason, Ben. Do not be distracted by the paid entertainment. Once we know Lady Rebecca Rutherford is safe, you can lift as many skirts as you please. I would also be cautious as to who has tupped the lady before you. Some of these gentlemen look quite dubious'

Alexander noticed that some of the ton's most notorious gentlemen were already in attendance.

How could a brother allow such men to be in the home they shared with their sister, doing the scandalous things that they were doing?

'I shall not be lifting any skirts this evening, or any other evening for that matter, my dear friend. I am a changed man. In fact, I have decided to find myself a wife.' Benjamin delighted at the shocked expression on the dukes' face.

'I do not believe it. I predict you will be fucking the redhead by dawn. In fact, we should wager on it,' Alexander laughed while shaking his head, rubbing his chin in disbelief.

'I most certainly will not, and I would be delighted to wager ten pounds to the contrary, my friend,' Benjamin grinned.

They shook hands to confirm the bet, the light-hearted banter suddenly interrupted by the booming voice of Robert Rutherford.

'Your Grace, Viscount Turner, welcome.' It was obvious that the earl was already in his cups, a glass in his hand as he greeted them. He wore no jacket or cravat, his shirt open at the neck, lifting his hand beckoning for them to follow him.

The room that they entered was well-lit with candles, the air filled with cigar and pipe smoke. A side table was laden with bottles of spirits. Men of varying ages filled the room, some already seated at card tables while others were greedily consuming the copious amounts of alcohol available to them.

The redhead that had passed them on arrival circled the room, while another woman in a similar state of undress sat on the lap of a younger man, his hand running up and down her leg as he nuzzled her neck.

There would have been a time not so long ago when Alexander would have revelled in such things, but as he stood taking in the view, not one of the vices on offer appealed to him more than Lady Rebecca Rutherford. She was within his reach and nothing he was witnessing right now would satisfy him in the way he knew she would. He had only kissed her, but those stolen moments had made him feel more alive than he had ever felt before. He needed to see her again so he could prove to himself that this was just a temporary infatuation and that he was not going to develop feelings for a lady who was far too unsuitable to be his Duchess.

'Your Grace, your Grace,' Benjamin spoke in hushed tones.

'I have told you not to call me that,' Alexander hissed.

'I had to get your attention somehow. You were wool gathering again. I am sure that was Flora walking down the hallway.' Benjamin nodded to the open doorway. 'I recognise her from promenading in the park. They are often together.'

The words had barely left Benjamin's mouth before the Alexander had hot-footed it out the door to catch up with the maid. Flora was hurrying along the hallway, aware that she was being followed. After Rebecca's recent experience, she began to feel more afraid as the footsteps got closer. The Earl's parties were becoming more frequent, with some of the younger female staff afraid to leave their quarters; at least one maid left her employment due to a terrifying encounter with an elderly lord.

'Miss, Miss, Flora ... Stop please.' Alexander had almost caught up with her now, unaware that she was now becoming panicked at his proximity.

'Please, my Lord. I need to be on my way.' On hearing her words, he now realised she was frightened.

'Stop please, I wish you no harm. I am here to help Lady Rebecca,' he said in a hushed tone.

At the mention of her mistress's name, Flora stopped, slowly turning to face the duke.

'I am sorry if I frightened you. It was not my intention. You know my sister, Lady Emma Fane? She is close friends with Lady Rebecca,' Alexander said.

Flora gasped before dropping to a curtsy. 'I apologise your Grace. You must forgive me, I did not recognise you there,' she replied, still breathless after her dash through the hallways.

'Flora, can you tell me which room Lady Rebecca is in? I need to speak with her. My sister has advised me she is concerned for the lady's safety. You must direct me to her whereabouts immediately.'

The maid did not know for sure whether the duke was sincere or he was just another unscrupulous gentleman wanting to dishonour Lady Rebecca. But something in his face seemed genuine. She had to trust him. 'Your Grace. The earl is keeping her like a prisoner until her wedding day. The door is always locked.'

'I assume that you have access to a key so you can attend to her?' Alexander was now becoming impatient, his tone of voice getting fraught.

'I do. But if his lordship knew I had given you the key, he would throw me on the street or worse. He is not a good man, your grace.' A single tear escaped her eye which she quickly wiped away with her sleeve.

Alexander bent forward slightly so that he was more level with Flora, placing a sympathetic hand on her shoulder. He had shocked both himself and Flora with the gentle gesture due to the differences in their stations. Aware that she feared what would happen if she were discovered, Alexander could not help but show the loyal maid some compassion.

'I will make sure you are protected, Flora. I give you my word,' he smiled before stepping back, removing his hand from her shoulder and returning to his imposing stature. 'I do not take pleasure in what I am about to say, but as a Duke, I must *insist* you give me the key and direct me to the lady's chamber at once.' Although he hated pulling rank, Alexander knew the maid would have to oblige.

Flora had no choice but to hand the key over to him; there were only two keys that she knew of, the earl keeping the other in his own chambers. Directing Alexander to the correct room, she stood for a moment, watching his back as he disappeared along the hall, hopeful that this would be the man to save Rebecca from a life of misery.

~

Holed up in her chambers, Rebecca sat nervously on the edge of her bed. It was going to be another long evening of depravity. For the past few hours, she had watched the comings and goings from her window. Earlier, her mind had started playing tricks when she thought she saw the Duke of Sandison alight from a carriage. This was inconceivable, due to him detesting Robert even more than she did; surely, he would never accept an invitation from her brother. She also did not like the idea that the duke partook in the kind of entertainment her brother provided.

Now dark outside, her reflection was visible in the windowpanes due to the various candles she had positioned around the room; she preferred her chamber to be well-lit in the evening so she could sit and devour her books. She could already hear crude laughter, the slamming of doors, and men cursing as they chased giggling women through the hallways.

As before, Rebecca had struggled to drag the chair against the door, fearful that her brother would turn a blind eye if a guest wanted to take liberties with her. He would probably just hand them the key to her room, especially if any money was offered for the privilege.

Trying to distract herself from what was happening around her, Rebecca picked up a book and sat on the chair that was now lodged against the door. She had barely read a passage when she was distracted by the sound of footsteps. Closing her book, she listened more intently, her heart racing as she realised the footsteps had stopped outside the door to her chambers. A few minutes passed before there was a gentle knock. Not realising she was holding her breath, she did not answer, hoping that they would go away. They knocked again.

Alexander had waited around the corner until there was no one about before he knocked on Rebecca's door. She had ignored it twice. He did not blame her; she was likely afraid of who it could be. He made sure the hallway was empty before he spoke in the most subdued tone he could manage.

'Rebecca. I know you are in there. I am going to unlock the door now.'

Rebecca once again thought she was imagining things - the voice sounded exactly like the Duke of Sandison. 'Your Grace, is that you?'

'Yes. I have a key, so I am going to come in now.' He retrieved the key from his pocket before placing it in the lock, making sure no one was watching him.

'Noo ohh, you cannot, not yet your Grace … One moment,' Rebecca squealed.

'I do not care if you are in your nightgown, my lady. We must be quick, before I am seen', he proceeded to turn the lock, but something was preventing him from entering.

'Why will the door not open? Let me in.'

'Aaaargh! Why do you not listen? I told you to wait a moment!' Rebecca was reminded how infuriating he could be.

The door was now slightly ajar, enough so he could look to see the offending item blocking the entrance. The gap started to open a little wider, allowing him to see Rebecca through the gap. She seemed to be using all the strength she had to push an armchair across the room.

He thought she looked both comical and magnificent. Her hair hung loose down her back in thick chestnut waves. Much longer than he had imagined, she wore nought but a white nightgown that clung beautifully to her rump, her bare feet slightly visible when she moved ungracefully across the floor while pushing the bulky piece of furniture. Alexander was now able to enter the room, closing and locking the door behind him. She still hadn't turned to look at him, busying herself with repositioning the chair. Alexander could not stop staring at her curvaceous form as she moved freely without the restrictions of cumbersome gowns and tightly strung undergarments. He longed for her to turn and face him.

'What on earth are you doing?' he asked.

'What does it look like, your Grace ... Moving the chair back,' Rebecca answered while rolling her eyes.

So impudent.

'I can see that, but why did you move it in the first place?' he asked.

Rebecca spun round so fast when he asked the question; he could not help but delight in the sight of her breasts bouncing against the light fabric of her night dress. Her pert nipples grazing the white cloth caused his cock to twitch at the spectacular sight before him.

'I have had some bother with a few unsavoury gentlemen as of late. I feel safer with the chair against the door. It is supposed to prevent entry.' Considering for a moment if she should cover herself with a robe due to the duke's lingering gaze, Rebecca decided not to bother, rather liking the way his eyes lazily travelled over her body.

'Why are you here, your Grace?' She tilted her head to the side, peering at him through curious eyes, thinking that he looked a little more roguish than usual.

'Your friends are very concerned for you. They have tried calling on you but are turned away. Since Emma received your note, she has not been herself, fretting constantly. She tells me you are like a sister to her. Every day she asks if I can do anything to help. I come out of concern for her.'

This was only part truth; unable to get Lady Rebecca out of his mind, he had also been desperate to see her again.

'Viscount Turner and I managed to secure invites rather easily for tonight. Your brother is quite happy to garner friends when he is on a winning streak,' Alexander said. 'Should they be concerned for you? Have you come to any harm, my Lady?'

'I can confirm that I am not dead in a ditch or lying with a bullet hole in my skull as Robert dances a happy jig, your Grace,' she replied sarcastically.

Rebecca was pleased that her friends cared enough for her that they needed proof she was well, but she was also slightly riled that Alexander had not come of his own accord after what had passed between them.

'I see that you continue to try and offend me with your choice of language, Lady Rebecca'.

Laughing at her comments, Alexander was far from being offended as he had been during earlier encounters with the young lady. He now found that he enjoyed her dramatic outbursts, although she most likely read too many inappropriate novels that caused her imagination to run a little wild.

The sight of the duke with a rakish smirk on his handsome face made Rebecca feel both annoyed and excited at the same time. 'Apart from being kept prisoner in my own home, not allowed to see or speak to anyone other than my maid. Having to barricade myself in for fear of attack. No, they should not be concerned … Oh, and being forced to marry a man I detest.' She rolled her eyes at what she had considered a stupid question.

Alexander did suppose his enquiry was a little thoughtless, but he didn't think it deserved such a severe response. 'You do not need to speak so harshly. I only wish to help.' Alexander knew that closing the distance between himself and a beautiful temptress in nothing but her nightdress was unwise. But he could not help himself. The desire to be closer to her was overwhelming.

'Do you not care for my welfare also, your Grace?' she hissed.

'Do not call me that, my name is Alexander. Alex, if you prefer.' He moved closer still, allowing his hand to brush against hers.

'You did not answer my question, *Alex*.' Her eyes never left his when she spoke his name.

The proximity to the woman who invaded his dreams every night made his breath quicken. He kept his hands fisted at his sides to stop himself from reaching out and pulling her into his arms. She was at her most vulnerable; he told himself he would not take advantage of the situation, no matter how much he needed to feel the softness of her body pressed to his.

'Of course, I care. I care very much,' Alexander insisted as he moved further forward.

She was standing so close now that he could feel the warmth emanating through her nightgown. To resist her now would be impossible. The look of need on her face and the way she was biting her cheek was an invitation to sin. And then she uttered two simple words. 'Show me'.

The sultry look that Rebecca gave him, along with the vision of the white fabric clinging to the soft curves of her body, was his undoing. It was not altogether clear who reached for who first but that did not matter to either of them; when their lips met, the kissing was frantic. Alexander held Rebecca firmly by the waist as she unashamedly tugged his hair, pulling him closer. With one hand in his hair, the other finding the lapels of his jacket eager to remove the garment, he quickly assisted in shrugging it off until it landed on the floor, swiftly followed by his cravat and waistcoat. His lips were now running a fiery trail down her neck, his large hand travelling from her slender waist before settling on her breast, his thumb gently stroking her hardened nipple as it strained against the nightgown. Slipping the crisp fabric from her shoulders, he kissed and licked the milky skin before lowering his head to take one of her nipples in his mouth through the warm fabric.

'Oh, Alex … I ….'

'What do you need Rebecca … What do you want?'

His mouth remained on her breasts, continuing to suck each nipple simultaneously, the fabric wet and transparent from his devouring tongue, his own groans of pleasure filling the room.

As his hands firmly grabbed her backside, his lips leaving a trail of desperate kisses over the swell of her breasts, she suddenly pulled away. Breathless and more aroused than he had ever been, Alexander took a step back, thinking that she had come to her senses and wanted this madness to stop. Rebecca was looking at him, her mouth slightly open as if she wanted to speak, her eyes never leaving him. Alexander was just about to end the silence when she did something he had not expected; she lifted her nightdress over her head and threw it to the floor.

Rebecca did not know if she would ever get the opportunity to be so daring again, especially if she was married to Lord Phillips. The way her body was responding to Alexander's touch was like nothing she could ever have imagined. She had explored her own body when alone at night, enjoying the sensation when she touched herself and the climaxes that followed but it had never felt as magical as what he was doing to her right now. The feel of his tongue through the fabric of her night clothes was glorious but she longed to feel his hands and mouth on her bare skin.

So overcome with desire for this beautiful man, she did not care if he would think her brazen or wanton at this moment; all she wished for was to feel his touch against her bare skin. She had slowly slipped off her nightgown, which had settled on the floor by her bare feet, and now stood fully naked in the candlelit room. Alexander had not said a word or even moved. He had just stared at her, his eyes studying every part of her needy body. Rebecca's heart was beating so fast she was sure he could hear it. Not wanting to seem nervous to a man of the duke's experience, all she could think to do was seductively adjust her long hair, allowing it to cascade over one shoulder. He was gazing at her in a way that made the ache between her thighs grow more desperate, his eyes darkening with desire as they searched every inch of her body.

'I need you to touch me.' She tried to sound confident when she spoke, but inside, she had never been so afraid; afraid he might reject her for being so sinful.

'Oh God, Rebecca. You are the most exquisite creature I have ever seen.' He reached out, cupping her face with his large hands before covering her mouth with his as he ran his fingers through her hair. His tongue ran along her lip, willing her to open her mouth wider until their tongues touched. Alexander groaned into Rebecca's eager mouth, pulling her closer, allowing her to feel his hard cock nestling against her hip. So consumed with passion, neither could recall when or how he had removed his shirt.

Rebecca drew back for a moment, arching her body so she could admire his broad chest and strong arms, running her fingers over the dark hair that trailed down his front. Her exploration had given Alexander the space and opportunity he needed to lower his head to her breasts. Rebecca purred as he rolled his wet tongue over her nipple, the panting and moaning sounds she was making encouraging him to take her nipple in his mouth and suck. Whispering his name while he sucked and caressed her breasts, he knew he had to taste her, scooping her up into his arms and smiling when she squealed in surprise.

'What are you doing Alex?' she giggled.

'Ravishing you', he nuzzled her neck with a sound of amusement in his voice.

~

As he lay Rebecca down on the bed, Alexander hovered over her while admiring her natural beauty, her cheeks were flushed, her hair wild as it cascaded over the pillows. Rebecca sat up, balancing on her elbows as she watched Alexander worshipping her body, any nervousness she had felt in her nakedness had soon evaporated when she had seen the look of lust in his eyes. Kissing her belly, his fingers stroking her thighs as he straddled her, Rebecca thought she might faint at the sensations she was feeling. He moved further down the bed, lifting her leg as he ran his tongue from her calf to hip encouraging her to part her legs for him. Lifting his head, his hand toying with the curls between her thighs, he looked up to see that Rebecca was watching him.

'Do you trust me, Rebecca?' he growled.

She nodded with a smile that would light up any room, a smile that took his breath away. When he slipped his tongue into her wetness, Rebecca had to put her hand over her mouth to muffle her screams. There were no words to describe the sensations overtaking her body, the way he was licking and kissing between her thighs should have made Rebecca blush, especially when Alexander grabbed her legs, hooking them over his shoulders so he could bury his face further into her core.

'Alex, I feel, I think ... Oh *yes*,' she cried.

Alexander thought he might spend in his trousers as Rebecca writhed beneath him, she was so wet and sensitive to everything he did, and now as she came apart on his tongue, all he wanted was to strip off his remaining clothes and drive his hard cock into her so she would be ruined for any other man.

~

Rebecca now lay on the bed completely sated; she covered her face with her hands as Alexander crawled up the bed to lie at her side. Smiling as he gently prised her hands away from her face, Alexander kissed Rebecca firmly on the mouth; she wantonly responded to the kiss, wrapping her arms around his neck the taste of her still on his soft lips.

As they lay facing each other in bed, Rebecca struggled to keep herself awake as Alexander stroked her naked back, her leg draped over him.

'I am afraid I must leave before suspicions arise. Ben can only distract your brother for so long', he said apologetically.

After kissing Rebecca on the tip of her nose, he reluctantly left her side, dressing as she watched him with sleepy eyes. Pocketing his cravat, Alexander returned to the edge of the bed, leaning down to place a chaste kiss on her cheek.

'Why do you always smell like lavender *your grace*?' she probed teasingly

Alexander was slightly taken aback at both her question and her use of his title after what they had been doing for the last hour.

'I bathe in lavender oil. It helps the pain I suffer in my back *my Lady*. Does the smell displease you?' he teased back.

'Oh no, *your Grace*. It pleases me very much. One day, I too would like to bathe in lavender oil,' she replied with a wink.

She would be the death of him with her naughty little remarks. The vision of her lying in his bath instantly made his cock go hard again. He could easily arrange for a bath large enough for two. Alexander could not bring himself to look away as Rebecca climbed from the bed with the counterpane wrapped around her nakedness strolling towards him; with her tangled hair trailing down her back, she looked marvellous. Alexander could not help grinning like a besotted fool as he admired the red marks visible on her bare shoulders, a reminder of his impassioned kisses.

'What are you doing, Rebecca. You should sleep.'

'I must pull the chair back. I would never be able to sleep thinking someone could come in', she fretted.

Rebecca's face was etched with worry as she held the bedcover close to her body, the look on her face was not one he would ever have expected from the audacious, brazen lady he had come to know. Alexander was experiencing feelings unfamiliar to him; it took all his resolve not to throw her over his shoulder and take her as far from here as he could. He needed to get out of her room fast, or he might never leave. Rebecca stood close enough so he could reach out to take hold of her wrist, allowing him to tenderly kiss the palm of her hand.

'Goodnight, *my Lady.*' Alexander's lips remained pressed to her palm as he bid her farewell.

'Goodnight *your Grace.*' Rebecca sighed as her body tingled at the gentle caress.

When the door closed behind him, the clicking sound of the key turning in the lock, Rebecca rested her back against the hard wood, pulling the covers tighter to her body, happier than she had been for a very long time.

CHAPTER THIRTEEN

With the sweet taste of Lady Rebecca still on his lips, Alexander made his way back to where he had left Benjamin, deliberately maintaining his unkempt appearance. Having returned the key to Flora, he was now pacing along the dark hallways, sounds of pleasure emanating from various rooms, with some doors remaining open, allowing guests to watch. Or join in. Men lay with men and women lay with women, the sweet smell of opium around every corner.

Alexander knew that Robert Rutherford did not treat his sister well, but for the first time he was witnessing the man's depravity and disregard for Rebecca's safety. Before tonight, Alexander had convinced himself she was just a passing infatuation, but when she had removed her night dress, revealing her perfect body to him, he had never wanted a woman more. Although she had tried to appear bold and brazen when baring herself to him, Alexander had seen the nervousness in her face, her hands shaking as they hung by her side. He did not speak in that moment as he took in the sight of her; if he were not a gentleman, he would have taken her innocence without a second thought. The duke felt both anger and jealousy at the thought of another touching and tasting her body as he had, especially the detestable Lord Phillips.

Alexander needed to erase his thoughts before re-entering the gaming room and continuing to play the part of the wicked duke they expected him to be. Ruffling his hair a little more, he casually strolled into the room.

'There you are Fane. Where the hell have you been?' Benjamin spoke quietly through gritted teeth, annoyed that he had been left alone with the earl and his unsavoury guests for so long. He was currently lounging back in his chair, the table in front of him strewn with coins, scribbled notes, and abandoned playing cards that were soiled from spilt alcohol.

'Got distracted,' was all Alexander could think to say, not wanting to catch his friend's eye.

Rutherford peered over his glass, his bloodshot eyes studying the duke as he went to sit in a vacant chair, noting Alexander's lack of cravat and rumpled jacket.

'Have you been tupping the staff your Grace? You look rather dishevelled. You have the look of a man that has been well and truly fucked, and it cannot have been one of the whores as they are all occupied.' The earl slurred as his eyes perused the room where women cavorted with drunken Lords.

Inside, Alexander was more than furious; he detested Rutherford, but had to continue the ruse, offering his host the best fake grin he could muster while pouring himself a large drink.

'A gentleman never tells,' he replied, taking a large swig of whisky, before refilling it with another.

'As I see no gentlemen in the room, you must tell all, your Grace,' an unknown voice announced. This came from further down the table from a man who had just joined the party, accompanied by the redheaded woman from earlier. It was a voice that Alexander did not recognise, the man obscured by the woman as she sat on his lap, his hands fondling her now bare breasts. Rutherford nodded his head in feigned amusement at the stranger's comment.

'You must tell me who the little whore is, your Grace, so I might have a go myself.' Laughing, the unknown man now had his hand under the woman's skirts while conversing with Alexander, his face still not visible.

'Is someone going to deal cards or are we here to discuss where I like to dip my cock?' Alexander hated speaking in such a course manner but needed to keep up the facade, trying not to look in Benjamin's direction, aware that his friend was sniggering at his foul words.

Rutherford looked in the direction of the man at the other end of the table while shuffling the fresh deck of playing cards. The woman was now adjusting her dress and removing herself from the man's lap, allowing Alexander a clear view of his face.

Phillips … What the hell?

Alexander kicked Benjamin under the table to garner his attention, the Viscount leaning over slightly so no one would be able to hear them speak.

'You just kicked me, and it was bloody painful.' Benjamin rubbed his calf as he glared at his friend.

'Apologies. I did not mean to kick you so hard but how long has Phillips been here?' whispered the duke.

'This is the first time that I have seen him this evening, slimy bastard. So, are you going to tell me where you have been all this time? I assume you spoke with the lady?' Benjamin enquired.

'Yes. We will speak of it later. She is quite well.'

Alexander wanted to quickly change the subject before Benjamin guessed what had transpired between them in Rebecca's bedchamber. Judging by the knowing look currently on the young viscount's face, he had already guessed. After playing another two games of cards and losing both, Alexander and Benjamin threw their hands up in defeat before bidding the other men at the table goodnight, Benjamin tossing his cards to the floor in fake anger.

~

Sitting back comfortably in the carriage on his way home, Alexander was relieved that everything had gone to plan, and much more. Both men's pockets were lighter after deliberately losing to Rutherford as part of the plan to keep in his favour. Alexander grinned as he listened to Benjamin lightly snoring and muttering while in an alcohol-induced sleep, glad of the peace, and not having to answer any prying questions regarding Lady Rebecca Rutherford.

CHAPTER FOURTEEN

Rebecca slept better than she had in days. Having woken naked, she had just called for a bath while Flora busied herself around the room. She was exhausted when the duke left, lacking the energy to drag her usual chair against the door, tiredness overwhelming her after so many sleepless nights. Rebecca stretched her arms above her head as she still lay abed, making a loud yawning sound to attract her maid's attention.

'Flora how are you this morning?' Rebecca knew that her maid could not ignore her for much longer. She had been watching her from bed, aware that Flora was avoiding looking at her. Rebecca felt herself start to blush, suddenly remembering that she was completely naked, her discarded nightdress now folded over the back of a chair. She pulled the covers over her head to hide her embarrassment just as Flora turned around to speak.

'I am fine, thank you for asking, my Lady. How are you? Did you sleep well?'

When the maid spoke, Rebecca thought she detected a hint of humour in her tone. 'I am going to come out from under the blankets now, Flora. You must not think badly of me. Do you promise?' Rebecca cagily pulled the covers to just below her chin.

'I could never think badly of you, my Lady. Is there something you would like to tell me?' Flora sat on the chair by the side of the bed with her hands clasped in her lap.

'Oh, Flora, I do not know where to begin. I fear I have made a huge mistake.'

Rebecca proceeded to tell Flora what had been happening between her and the duke over the past weeks, sparing her the more salacious details.

~

Alexander had not slept well the night before. His skin was pale, and he had dark circles below his eyes. He had lain awake most of the night considering his feelings for Lady Rebecca Rutherford, his cock stiffening as he recalled the sounds she made when he had touched her.

He slowly washed himself with the fresh cloth that had been soaking in the basin of warm water, unwilling to wash the scent of Rebecca from his skin too quickly. Once he had finished his morning ablutions, he made his way to breakfast. His mother and sister were already seated at the table, quietly conversing. The peacefulness of the room pleased him greatly due to his pounding headache.

'Good morning, my darling boy. What on earth have you been up to? You look utterly dreadful.' The Dowager Duchess put down her teacup as she looked her son up and down.

Alexander grunted in response. 'Bad decisions mother, bad decisions.'

Although not all bad.

'Do tell, brother,' Emma pried.

Alexander gave his sister a disapproving look as he began buttering the warm toast. He knew that he must tell Emma he had spoken with Rebecca, but also needed time to compose himself. He feared that his growing feelings for the lady and what had transpired in her bedchamber might be evident on his face, especially to his mother.

~

After eating a hearty breakfast of eggs and bacon, washed down with numerous cups of coffee, Alexander started to feel his stomach settling, albeit a little tired as he sat trying to make sense of the various ledgers on the desk before him. The sound of women's voices and approaching footsteps signalled that his mother and sister were once again about to intrude on his solitude.

'Alexander, may we come in?' The Dowager didn't wait for an answer as she sashayed into the room, closely followed by her sprightly daughter.

'What do you want? You can see that I am quite busy?' He pointed to the stack of books on his desk.

'Alexander, you do know that servant's talk, dear?' Evelyn said softly.

'Yes, I am aware,' Alexander replied to his mother. Knowing where this conversation was going, he felt his headache returning.

'Those bad decisions that you made last evening; did they involve Lady Rebecca Rutherford?'

'MOTHER, what are you talking about?! What have you heard?' Alexander did not mean to speak to the dowager in such a blunt manner and quickly apologised.

'Brother, we know that you were at the Earl of Fordew's home with that *awful* friend of yours, doing all sorts last night,' Emma scolded.

'Emma, we were not doing *all sorts*, as you suggest ... and what do you know of such things?'

Emma rolled her eyes and let out a long sigh.

'Children, children, no quarrelling *please*', Evelyn smiled at each of her children, her gaze lingering on her son for longer, willing him to admit what he had been up to.

'It is not what you think.' He directed his words to his mother, aware that he could not avoid any more probing questions from the formidable Scotswoman. Moving away from his desk, Alexander sat in the large armchair next to the fireplace, his long legs stretched out in front of him. Now that he had both ladies' attention, the duke began to explain the plan that himself and Benjamin had concocted to gain access to the earl's home and to ascertain the whereabouts of Lady Rebecca Rutherford.

'Well, well, that is quite the ruse, dear,' the Dowager Duchess eyed Alexander curiously after he had finished talking.

'Thank you, brother. It is of some comfort to know that Rebecca is quite well,' Emma smiled.

She was very well indeed when I was between her thighs.

Alexander feigned a cough as he tried to erase the picture of her naked body wrapped around him.

Emma swiftly left the room, muttering something about letting her friends know *right away*, leaving him on his own with his mother.

Alexander was feeling slightly uncomfortable as his mother glared at him. Waiting for her to speak, he nervously began crossing and uncrossing his feet, feeling like a young boy again waiting to be scolded for some misdemeanour.

'Alexander, you have feelings for the girl?' his mother asked sympathetically.

Alexander had not expected *that*; he thought she was going to lecture him on drinking and gambling with reprobates like Robert Rutherford.

'Do not be absurd,' he scoffed.

'I know you, Alexander. You have feelings for her.'

Running his fingers through his hair, he really did not know what to say; he could not lie to his mother.

'I think I might be developing a fondness for the lady. I am sure it is just a passing infatuation; she can be quite maddening.' He could not look at his mother as he confessed.

Standing, the Dowager walked over to her son placing a hand on his shoulder. 'I suspect this is much more than a mere infatuation, but that is only the opinion of a romantic old woman, my dear.' She walked towards the open door, stalling momentarily when the duke called out.

'Mother. Please do not mention any of this to Emma.'

The Dowager nodded her head and smiled before heading up to her room, hopeful that her beloved son might marry for love after all.

CHAPTER FIFTEEN

Rebecca had just finished lunch in her chambers when the door flew open. Robert marched in looking even more bedraggled than normal, Flora at his back. Before she could comment on him entering without knocking, he had her by the arm, attempting to drag her from where she sat at the small writing desk.

'Come with me,' he demanded. 'Your sister has had the child. We depart today.'

'You allow me to leave the house, Robert?' Rebecca was confused as to the sudden announcement.

'Unfortunately, I do not have a choice in the matter. It would cause much talk amongst the ton if you did not visit Rose after the birth of her child, and we do not wish *that*. Now, hurry up. We leave within the hour.'

Robert Rutherford then left the room as quickly as he had entered. Having been advised by the earl to pack enough belongings for three days, Flora began gathering some of Rebecca's items in readiness for loading into her trunk. As Rebecca watched Flora dashing about the room, she suddenly remembered the maid's clothing that she had hidden.

While the servants were rushing around, packing trunks and readying carriages, Rebecca managed to slip away to scribble a quick note to Emma, before discreetly passing this to a loyal footman for delivery. She was standing at the top of the staircase, eager to leave, when she saw Robert standing at the bottom, impatiently tapping his foot. She had not considered that he might be going with her, hopeful that she would be rid of him for a few days.

Thankfully, the carriage ride to Rose's house was only a few hours' drive. Being in such a confined space with Robert was anything but ideal, as he spent most of the journey swigging from a flask that he kept in his breast pocket. Rebecca tried to avoid her brother's scowling face; when he drank spirits, his unstable temperament would grow even worse. She caught his eye on a couple of occasions and could tell that he was in the mood for an argument, quickly diverting her gaze to watch the surrounding landscapes through the carriage window.

Arriving at the estate where her sister Rose lived with her husband, Sir Thomas Redpath and their children, Robert immediately disembarked from the carriage, shoving the approaching footman out of his way. Rebecca could tell that the young footman was shocked, if not enraged, by her brother's behaviour, his hands shaking slightly as he assisted her from the carriage.

'I am so very sorry about him. My brother can be quite the ass.' The footman was taken aback when Rebecca spoke to him in such a kind manner, especially at her choice of language when describing the rude gentleman that had nearly knocked him to the ground.

Rose's home had always felt welcoming. The family had a good relationship with all the staff they employed; Rebecca could not help feeling more cheerful than she had been of late. She was led into the drawing room where her sister sat cradling the new babe, her husband by her side. Rosalind was standing by the window talking with Robert who was already holding a full glass of brandy. There was something different in the viscountess's expression as she spoke to him, a look that Rebecca had never seen from her sister. Rosalind appeared utterly furious. When Rebecca walked into the room after assessing the scene in front of her, Rosalind turned to greet her, leaving Robert standing on his own.

'Rebecca dear, how lovely to see you.' Rosalind took her sister's hand while kissing her on the cheek.

Rebecca wondered if her sister knew that she had been forbidden to leave her room, locked in like a prisoner. She considered saying something, but not wishing to spoil Rose's happy day, now was not the time.

Rose patted the seat next to her for Rebecca to sit, before placing the newborn in her arms.

'Meet your nephew, George.' Rose looked at her baby then back to her husband, who was adoringly watching his wife.

Observing the interaction between the couple, Rebecca felt sad that she would never have what they had. Cradling baby George in her arms confirmed to her just how much she desired a child of her own one day, wishing it would be born out of love and not duty.

Rebecca was thoroughly enjoying the day with her family, she had been happily playing in the garden with her beloved nieces when Robert appeared at her side. The smell of alcohol emanating from him was quite nauseating.

'Enjoying your freedom are you *sister*', he sneered, quite unsteady on his feet.

'Go away and sober up, Robert. You will frighten the girls.' She attempted to elbow him away without the young children noticing.

'I am here to inform you that the date has been set for your wedding to Phillips. Two weeks from today,' he slurred, almost gleefully.

Rebecca's heart sank. What had been a lovely day had now turned out to be one of the worst days of her life; she now feared she may never be able to escape this marriage to Lord Phillips after all.

'Did you deliberately wait until today to inform me of this, deliberately spoiling everything?' she snapped back.

'You know me so well, but you might want to speak with dear Rosalind about the arrangements. Hearty congratulations, sister.' Laughing and muttering to himself, Robert staggered off in the direction of the house.

~

Alexander was about to enter his townhouse when a footman arrived, holding a letter addressed to his sister, which he accepted before going in. Emma was so engrossed in the novel she was reading that she failed to notice Alexander stroll into the room, the Dowager napping on her chair in the corner, unfinished embroidery on her lap.

'Emma, this has been delivered for you.' Uninterested in its contents, he handed her the letter before taking the newspaper and sitting on one of the plump sofas.

'This is Rebecca's writing.' Putting her book to the side, Emma carefully unfolded the missive.

Alexander sat up straighter, looking over the news sheet at his sister as she read her friend's correspondence. When she eventually put the letter down and said nothing, Alexander's curiosity took over.

'Emma, has something happened?' He tried to keep his voice low while their mother slept, not wanting to disturb her.

'She has been taken to her sister, Rose's home to meet the new child; the earl insisted as he thought suspicions may be raised if she did not attend her sister after the birth.'

'That is a good thing, is it not?' Alexander was already considering how he could see her again.

'Yes, it may be a chance for me to visit her. Surely, I would not be refused entry by her sister and Sir Thomas,' Emma smiled while re-reading the missive.

'Sir Thomas Redpath is a fine gentleman. I would be very surprised if he was aware of Rutherford's treatment of his sister,' her brother added.

'I must go as soon as possible, then. Mother may wish to chaperone me; you know how she adores babies.' Emma was quite excited at the thought of seeing her best friend.

'I shall accompany you, to ensure you are safe. I do not trust Rutherford if he is there.' Alexander would go whether Emma wanted him to or not. 'We shall travel first thing tomorrow morning,' he declared.

'That will give me time to purchase a gift for the babe. We do not want the real reason for our visit to be known. It is likely that Rebecca's sisters do not know what Robert has been up to.'

Emma stood to leave, more elated than she had been for some time. Alexander watched his sister exit the room. He could not help but smile at the thought of seeing Rebecca the following day, when he heard his mother stirring.

'That is a beautiful smile, Alexander.' The Dowager had one eye open as she teased her son. 'You must decide if you want to be with Lady Rebecca Rutherford or you will lose her forever,' she stated before closing her eyes again and continuing to nap.

Taken aback at his mother's words, Alexander did not know how to answer her, although he knew that she was right. He needed to admit his feelings to himself before deciding what to do next.

~

Rebecca could not stop thinking about her brother's words and what he meant when he mentioned Rosalind and the *arrangements*. Returning indoors to look for her sister, Rebecca headed back to the drawing room. Conveniently, Rosalind was the only one in the room as Rose had retired to her bedchamber to rest before dinner. Robert was likely asleep or continuing to drink himself into oblivion somewhere else in the manor.

When Rebecca entered the room, the Viscountess looked up from the book she had been reading. 'Rosalind, can I speak with you?' Rebecca sat in the chair nearest to her sister.

'Of course, dear. Is something troubling you?' Rosalind asked as she put her book on the table at the side of her chair.

Trying not to sound aggrieved, Rebecca told her sister what Robert had said to her in the garden, asking her what he had meant; also mentioning the look of annoyance on her sister's face when she saw her talking with Robert earlier. Rosalind tilted her head to one side as if she did not know what Rebecca meant as she listened.

'Rebecca, I am sure you were mistaken. I was merely vexed at your brother's drinking, that had nothing to do with you.' The Viscountess almost sounded sincere.

'What he spoke of in the garden ... did you know that arrangements had been made for me to marry Lord Phillips in two weeks time?'

'Of course, she bloody did!' The booming voice alerted them to Robert who had materialised, as if magically, and was now casually leaning against the door frame.

Rebecca looked at her brother and sister, that same look of annoyance on Rosalind's face she had witnessed previously, as Robert sneered back at her.

'Brother, you are drunk', the Viscountess spoke through gritted teeth.

'What does he mean, Rosalind?', Rebecca asked.

'Can you not see he is drunk sister; he does not know what he is saying?' Rosalind fanned her hand dismissively in the direction of her brother.

Robert laughed, now supporting himself against the wall. 'It is about time our little sister knew how important her elder sister's reputation is within the ton.'

'I do not understand.' Rebecca looked at Rosalind, desperate for an answer, but it was her brother that spoke first.

'The viscountess is desperate for you to marry as soon as possible, before the scandal sheets report on my indiscretions and bring shame on the family name.'

For a man who had drunk so much, Robert was very clear in what he was revealing to Rebecca.

'Is this true?' Rebecca felt tears welling. She did not always get on with her eldest sibling but never thought she would put her reputation before the happiness of her own sister.

'It is not as you think,' she answered.

'What should I think, Rosalind?' Rebecca could see that Robert was enjoying every minute of the altercation taking place between his siblings.

'You should be grateful to your sister,' Robert said to Rebecca.

'And why is that, *dear brother?*' Rebecca was getting madder by the minute.

'I would have kept you locked in your chamber until you were safely at the altar. Rosalind was the one that convinced me to let you come here today,' Robert snarled.

'Because you did not want to raise suspicion within your precious ton.' Rebecca had not allowed herself to cry in front of them, her initial sadness at the situation now turning to anger.

'You do not understand how hard it has been for me to keep this family together, Rebecca. Robert has all but destroyed our good name.'

'Yes, Rosalind. *Robert* has destroyed it, *not* me, although it is *me* that must pay for his recklessness.'

'Do not be so dramatic, Rebecca. You are one and twenty. You should have been married by now. You should be thanking us.' Robert now sat on the sofa with his legs splayed out in front of him, looking ready to fall asleep.

'You do realise that Robert is right for once. You are of an age where you should be betrothed, if not married. You will be considered a spinster soon and then who will have you?'

'*Have* me?'

Rebecca did not think she could take any more as she shouted the words back at her sister. Not able to believe what she was hearing from them both, willing herself not to scream out loud, Rebecca could not stand being in the room a moment longer after hearing her sister's cruel words.

As she got up from her chair while avoiding looking at Rosalind, she passed where her brother sat with his eyes now closed. Unable to stop herself, she kicked him hard in the leg, taking satisfaction at the sound of him wincing, which was the last thing she heard as she stormed from the room.

CHAPTER SIXTEEN

It had been decided that Lady Matilda Brookfield should accompany Emma and Alexander when they visited Rebecca. With Matilda being the daughter of a duke, along with the Duke of Sandison himself, it was doubtful that they would be turned away. It was not the done thing to appear without invitation, but they did not want to risk Robert sending Rebecca away before they could talk to her.

Alexander sat opposite his sister and her friend for the carriage journey, grateful that the young ladies talked quietly, whispering to each other for most of the journey. Knowing his sister, they were probably plotting some grand rescue attempt that would involve hitting Rutherford over the head with an expensive vase or similar object.

Due to the evenings that Alexander and Benjamin had spent in the company of Robert Rutherford, it was important that he kept up the pretence of being a debauched scoundrel if he encountered the earl during this impromptu visit, which might be awkward, if not embarrassing, in front of Emma. He had to say something.

'Emma, I need to tell you something. Do not laugh, just listen please,' Alexander grimaced.

Emma leaned forward, as did her friend, keen to know what the duke was about to say.

'I will not go into great detail ladies. But Robert Rutherford thinks that I am something of a scoundrel and libertine.'

Emma laughed heartily before quickly lifting her hand to cover her mouth when she saw her brother frowning.

'And why on earth would he think that Alex?' she grinned, looking him up and down questionably.

'I will not discuss it further; I just wanted to warn you that if I behave differently in the Earl's company, please act as if it is perfectly normal.'

Alexander could see that his sister was desperate to interrogate him, a sly look in her eyes as she sat back in her seat.

'Please just do as I ask Emma,' he continued before she could speak.

Alexander was glad when they arrived at their destination, the ladies had chattered continuously throughout the journey, often glancing in his direction making it quite obvious that they were speaking about him.

Now, as they exited the carriage, he did not know if he was nervous or excited to see Rebecca again. They had not seen or spoken to each other since the evening in her bedchamber. He needed to know if what he was feeling was genuine affection or lust for the lady, his mother's words firmly lodged in his head playing over and over again … *You will lose her forever.*

~

Rebecca had decided to take her breakfast alone in her room when she woke up. Still unable to bear the company of her brother and sister after yesterday's revelations, she now stood in the library surrounded by bookshelves trying to decide on what to read.

She was aware of voices coming from the hall, assuming that more of her sister's friends had come to congratulate her on the birth of George. Finally deciding on a book of poetry as there were none of her favourite novels, she was disturbed by a gentle knock on the library door, before a young maid entered informing Rebecca that Rose had requested her company in the drawing room. Rebecca was slightly peeved as she had really wanted to be alone today but could not refuse the invitation. This was her sister's home, after all.

Nearing the drawing room, Rebecca began to recognise the voices coming from inside, praying that she was not imagining things she moved faster towards the room.

As Rose was seated facing the open door, she had seen Rebecca enter before Emma and Matilda who were both sitting facing the window. They both turned when they heard Rebecca's shriek.

'Emma … Matilda … You came! How I have missed you both,' she cried.

The young ladies could not contain their excitement in seeing Rebecca, leaping from their chairs to envelop her in a warm embrace.

When they had arrived, Alexander had asked to meet with Sir Thomas, a gentleman that he had met on a few occasions and got along with quite well. He longed to see Rebecca, but it would not be wise to see her just yet without raising suspicions as to why he would want to join a group of ladies cooing over a new baby. He also knew that when he saw her, he would not be able to take his eyes off her, which would surely not go unnoticed.

Alexander was enjoying a whisky with Sir Thomas in his study while they discussed their various businesses and what they had been doing of late, Thomas obviously besotted with his wife and children. Alexander rarely associated with men who were genuinely in love with their wives and felt a sense of jealousy when Thomas spoke so fondly of his expanding family. Alexander had witnessed his own parents' love for each other but had never considered that he himself would marry for love. Since inheriting his title, he had become more concerned with marrying a lady that would perform the duties required of a Duchess and birthing an heir to continue the family line, not even considering a love match. Alexander surprised himself as he immediately recoiled at the thought of Rebecca married to someone other than him, conjuring the disturbing vision of her heavy with another man's child.

~

Rose soon excused herself, leaving the three ladies alone in the drawing room, closing the door behind her, allowing them some privacy to chat. It was then that Rebecca realised her sister Rose was nothing like the other siblings. The two sisters never had much of a chance to get to know each other growing up due to their difference in age, but now Rebecca could see her sister was kind and caring in her own way.

'How have you been Rebecca? What is going on?' Emma asked as soon as the door was firmly closed.

Rebecca began to reveal details of her brother's sordid parties, drawing gasps from the ladies as well as curious questions. She told them how she was afraid to be in her own home as strangers lurked in the dark corners of the hallways, and she also told them she was to be married in two weeks time.

'Two weeks!' Matilda said louder than she had anticipated.

'Yes, two weeks. I cannot see any way out of this now, Matilda,' Rebecca wept, unable to hide her tears from her friends.

Alexander was sitting in Thomas Redpath's study when Rebecca's sister Rose glided in, with a huge smile directed to her husband. Alexander thought there was quite the family likeness, but Rose did not have the same delightful gap between her front teeth and her eyes looked as if they were a dark shade of blue rather than green like Rebecca's. When both men got up out of their chairs as she entered the room, Rose dramatically shooed at them both to remain seated although they both stood anyway. Thomas instantly went to his wife, placing his hand on her lower back, her belly still rounded from her recent pregnancy. She looked at Alexander waiting for an introduction.

'Rose, I must introduce you to his Grace, the Duke of Sandison.'

'Your Grace, it is a pleasure to welcome you to our home. What brings you here today?' Rose enquired.

'I am accompanying my sister, Lady Emma Fane, and her good friend Lady Matilda Brookfield; I thought it would also be an excellent opportunity to catch up with your husband while the ladies converse in the drawing room as it has been some time since we have seen each other.' He decided not to mention Lady Rebecca as it was getting harder to speak her name without smiling.

'My sister is very lucky to have such wonderful friends, your Grace. You must know my youngest sister, Lady Rebecca Rutherford do you not?'

Alexander could have happily said that he knew the lady very well indeed but did not want to risk his expression giving away too much. He decided that it was best to just nod his head while muttering the words *I do*. The memory of her naked body arching beneath him would surely cause his cock to thicken in full view of the couple in front of him, which would be rather embarrassing to say the least.

'She is a very sweet girl, if not a little *exuberant* at times. I imagine your sister is of a similar character for them to be such good friends?' Sir Thomas smiled while puffing on the pipe that he had just lit.

'There is never a dull moment when Emma is around,' Alexander replied.

The polite conversation was interrupted when there was a loud crashing sound followed by a piercing yell from somewhere within the house. Suddenly, the house seemed to be in uproar. Rose, Thomas, and Alexander all looked at each other in confusion before rushing out of the room in the direction of the disturbance.

A few of the servants were already standing at the foot of the stairs as if they did not know what to do, while a well-dressed woman who looked very much like Rose was ordering someone to call for a doctor.

Alexander guessed that the woman taking charge of the situation was the eldest of the three sisters whose name he had forgotten; although very beautiful there was something about her countenance that was unlike that of Rebecca and Rose. Not knowing if he could be of any help, Alexander held back when Rose and Sir Thomas had raced ahead. Seconds later, one of the doors off the hallway flew open so fast it caused Alexander to jump, before he saw a vision in pale yellow run from the room in the direction of where the commotion was taking place. Alexander thought his heart was about to jump out of his chest when he saw Rebecca lift her hems and scurry to where her family were gathering, her chestnut hair tumbling down her back as her hips swayed when she moved. When the servants stepped aside, Alexander could see that it was Robert Rutherford, the Earl of Fordew, who lay still at the bottom of the staircase.

Sir Thomas quickly took charge of the situation; as a naval captain he was not unfamiliar with injury or accident, immediately ordering the servants to leave the earl where he lay until the doctor arrived.

Rebecca had been enjoying catching up with her friends when they were all startled by the noise coming from outside the room. Throwing open the door, she had rushed to see what was going on, Emma and Matilda not far behind, slightly afraid of what she might encounter, concerned that Rose or one of the children had taken a tumble down the stairs.

Sir Thomas and the butler were now huddled together assessing what had happened. Rebecca could just about make out that someone was lying completely still on the hard floor. It took her a few moments before she realised that it was her own brother lying unresponsive at the bottom of the staircase.

Alexander continued to watch Lady Rebecca as she stood with her two sisters watching the events unfold. A blanket had now been placed over the earl and he looked as if he was beginning to stir. Alexander decided that if he wanted to be near her, he would have to offer his assistance, although if the earl was never to awaken again it would still be too soon as far as he was concerned. Striding forward until he was standing beside Rebecca, the duke tried to sound concerned when he asked if he could be of help.

Rebecca immediately knew that Alexander Fane was standing beside her the moment she smelt the familiar scent of lavender invading her senses. Continuing to look straight ahead, afraid that it would not be him and just a figment of her imagination, she could only think of two words to say. 'You came.'

Alexander had to touch her. He did not feel the need to embrace or ravish her like he had done before, he just needed to feel even the gentlest caress of her skin against his. Moving slightly closer, Alexander lightly brushed his hand against hers and felt her shiver slightly before she cautiously moved her fingers until they were entwined with his. That was when they turned to look at each other. They stood gazing into each other's eyes for a few seconds, their hands laced together, forgetting for a moment that they were not alone before reluctantly parting when they heard a gasp from behind them.

Rebecca and Alexander had a good idea who had made the sound before they turned around and they were right. Emma stood with one hand over her mouth while the other was positioned theatrically against Matilda's arm as if she might faint. Due to the wicked glint in her eye and Lady Matilda's giggling, it was obvious that Emma may not be as shocked by what she witnessed as they thought.

Dr James Fleming was quite the dashing gentleman, a dark haired, bearded Scotsman well respected in his field, although not much older than thirty years. Unlike many of his profession, he welcomed new treatments and immersed himself in the most up-to-date medical journals, reading about pioneering treatments.

Not long after he arrived, the Earl had opened his eyes. Drifting in and out of consciousness, in obvious pain, he began to demand the doctor give him laudanum. The doctor was now on his knees trying to calm him down while checking him over, speaking to his patient firmly as he made demands of him. The remaining servants that had been assisting Sir Thomas had been excused when the doctor arrived, while Rose had escorted Rebecca and her friends to the drawing room where they now relaxed after the shock of Roberts accident.

Rebecca could not bring herself to look at Emma or Matilda who were sitting opposite her, awkward and embarrassed that they had caught her in an intimate moment with the duke, although happily chatting with Rose she could tell they were dying to get her alone. When the door opened and Alexander walked in with Sir Thomas, she knew that her two friends were watching, gauging her reaction.

After greeting the ladies, Alexander stood with his hands behind his back, trying not to look at Rebecca but failing miserably. The men had come to inform them that the servants were making up a bed in one of the downstairs rooms for Robert as he had broken both of his legs in the fall. Rose was the only one in the room showing genuine sympathy for the earl; her husband did not seem to share her concern. Rebecca could not help thinking that it served him right after the way he had been treating her.

'How is he? Is he awake, Thomas?' Rose asked.

'He has been given some laudanum for the pain my love. He will sleep 'til morning.' Thomas squeezed his wife's shoulder as she looked up at him, turning her head gently to kiss his hand.

Rebecca was surprised at her sister's behaviour towards her husband, especially as they were in company, and felt quite envious at their obvious love for each other. Sir Thomas tentatively removed his hand from Rose's shoulder when a servant knocked on the door to advise him the doctor was getting ready to leave. Bidding the guests farewell, Sir Thomas left the room to consult with Dr Fleming.

'Emma, Lady Matilda, I think it is time for us to leave. It has been a very difficult day for the family', Alexander announced.

Rebecca was sad to see her friends leave but also relieved that she would not have to explain what they had witnessed between her and the duke. She needed time to think.

When the carriage arrived, Alexander informed Emma that he would be travelling separately as he was going straight to his club due to a prior engagement. Emma watched him with narrowed eyes, not convinced he was being entirely truthful. Like her mother, the dowager duchess, Emma was highly intuitive, and Alexander was sure she saw right through his lie. But he needed to talk with Rebecca and had seen her enter a room at the far end of the hallway on her own.

When Alexander saw that the carriage was almost out of sight, he dashed back into the house, fearful that Rebecca may have gone elsewhere. Checking that he had not been seen re-entering the house, he practically sprinted along the hall, then quietly opened the door.

Rebecca spun round and let out a small squeak when she saw Alexander sail through the door, her delicate hand pressed to her heart. She had come to the parlour to consider what had happened to her brother and how it might affect her impending wedding. Robert had no way to control her while bedridden as he recovered from his accident; Rosalind, on the other hand, could be a problem.

Alexander closed the door at his back. Crossing the room, he wore a rakish smirk on his face as if he was about to devour every part of her body.

'Your Grace, you should not be here', Rebecca protested, her hand still placed against her beating heart.

'Is that so, my Lady?' He was now close enough to pull her into his arms.

'Anyone could walk in, Alex,' she said breathily.

The sound of his given name on her lips made his cock instantly hard. He held her tightly around the waist before kissing her passionately on the mouth. Guiding her until her back was against the wall, he dragged his mouth along her jaw before running his tongue down her throat as she sighed with desire. Rebecca wrapped her arms around his neck, kissing him back with as much vigour delighting in the feel of his hand as it travelled from her waist to her breasts. Rebecca withdrew from the kiss for a moment so she could lean back and watch his skilful hands as they caressed her breasts, his fingers running along the top of her décolletage before dipping beneath the fabric.

'God, Rebecca, I need to touch you … I need to feel your bare skin,' he groaned.

'I need you to touch me Alex,' she begged.

'Are you wet for me, Rebecca?' he panted.

Rebecca felt herself blushing at his words. She adored it when he acted like a rogue. It made her feel even more wanton, igniting feelings in her body she never thought possible.

'Are you? Tell me', he growled, trailing kisses down her neck, gently nipping her shoulder with his teeth.

Rebecca tried to answer in a sultry manner but all she managed was a high pitched, '*Yes*.' She could feel the duke smiling at her reply while he continued to devour her neck with his lips and tongue.

When their mouths clashed again with frenzied kisses, Alexander felt Rebecca's hand sliding down his front until she timidly stroked his swollen cock over his trousers. His own hand was now under her skirts exploring the soft skin above her stocking.

'Jesus Christ, Rebecca. We need to stop this,' Alexander groaned when her hand continued to rub up and down his rock-hard shaft as she giggled at his choice of language.

Grudgingly, he removed Rebecca's hand, raising it to his lips, gently kissing her wrist as he removed his hand from under her skirts.

'Sorry, I, I do not know how to please a man … Did I do something wrong?' she could not look at him as she apologised.

Alexander placed his hand beneath her chin, forcing her to look at him, thinking how adorable she was when she blushed.

'Please do not be sorry, my beautiful girl. You please me more than you could ever imagine. I am finding it more and more difficult to control myself when we are together,' he replied with a smile.

He then leaned down, playfully rubbing his nose against hers, kissing her on the forehead before reluctantly releasing her from his embrace. Smoothing down his ruffled hair and straightening his coat, he headed to the closed door, looking over his shoulder at the woman who had turned his life upside down. 'I shall sort this Rebecca', he said before he opened the door and left.

Rebecca sat down, her head in her hands, wondering what his words had meant and what he was going to do.

~

Alexander had taken his carriage to Whites so he would not rouse any more suspicion from his sister. He knew that Benjamin would be there, and he needed a drink. He did not know exactly what he meant when he had told Rebecca that he would *sort* it but sort it he would. His feelings for her were growing stronger by the day and he could not imagine another woman making him feel the way she did. It was all starting to get very complicated indeed.

The club was quieter than usual. Only a handful of gentlemen were in attendance, so it did not take him long to see Benjamin holding court with an older man that Alexander did not know. He decided not to interrupt him when he was in full flow, animatedly talking with his hands, which was a sure sign that he was drunk. Alexander took a seat in the corner, enjoying the solitude as he downed another whisky when his friend saw him and sauntered over.

'Fane, are you trying to hide from me?' Benjamin said a bit too loudly while collapsing into the chair opposite.

'As always', Alexander joked while pouring himself another large drink.

'You look quite sombre this evening my friend'

'I have just returned from accompanying my sister to visit Lady Rebecca Rutherford. It has been quite the day.'

Alexander told Benjamin about Robert Rutherford's accident, as well as Emma and Matilda witnessing the intimate scene between himself and Lady Rebecca. The young viscount listened intently while the duke spoke, occasionally nodding or shaking his head, causing his untamed hair to become even more unruly.

'So, you and Lady Rebecca?' Benjamin enquired curiously.

'I do not know Ben; I really do not know.'

'Might you be in love with the lady?'

Alexander was quite taken aback as he had not expected his friend to be so forthright in his questioning. He did not answer, afraid to admit out loud that his friend may be correct in his assumption.

~

Rebecca had just blown out the candle by her bed. She had tried to read her book but was so distracted she had re-read the same lines repeatedly, her thoughts continually returning to the duke. The idea of another man making her feel the way he did was impossible to imagine. When she had seen him standing in the hallway, her heart nearly jumped from her chest. He had looked so brooding and handsome when he gazed at her; he always seemed so stoic on the outside, but she had seen a different side to him, a playful, caring side. Lying in the darkness, Rebecca wondered what she should do. Whatever it took, she would *never* marry Phillips, no matter what scandal it brought to the family.

~

Alexander considered taking his breakfast alone in his study or waiting for his sister to return to her chambers, but he could not avoid her forever. She had probably written a list of questions to ask regarding Rebecca. Walking into the breakfasting room, Emma looked up with a glint in her eye as he had predicted. When he pulled out his chair at the head of the table her eyes never left him for a second, even as she took a nibble of her toast.

'Good morning brother. Did you sleep well?' Emma asked.

'Very well, thank you, sister.' If truth be told, he had not slept well at all.

Before she could interrogate him further, they heard the rustling of skirts and the dowager's voice as she briefly spoke to the butler before gliding through the doorway.

'Good morning children. I do believe I overslept.' She took a seat across from her daughter, aware of the silence between Alexander and Emma. 'Emma dear, have you plans for today? I thought we might take a trip to town. I am in need of some new gloves.'

'That would be nice, mother'

'And you, Alexander?' Evelyn asked her son.

The duke was not paying attention; his thoughts were elsewhere, so had not heard his mother's question.

'Alex!' Emma was close enough to kick her brother under the table to get his attention.

'Bloody hell, Emma. What did you do that for?' he chastised.

'Mother is speaking to you. Stop day dreaming and pay attention.' Emma replied. 'And mind your language, you are not at *Whites* now.'

As she took a sip from her teacup, the dowager duchess sniggered at the interaction between the two siblings.

'How was your visit with Rose Redpath and Rebecca yesterday? I was informed this morning that the earl took a tumble and broke both of his legs. How unfortunate for the young man.' Evelyn could not have sounded more insincere.

'Pity it was not his neck', Emma mumbled.

'Lady Emma Fane. You must not say things like that', Alexander chastised his sister, although he agreed with the sentiment entirely.

'Oh, Alex, do not deny that you think the same. I saw how you were with Rebecca yesterday, the way you looked at each other. You were holding her hand, for goodness sake.'

There it was. She had obviously been desperate to say it and he had walked right into her trap. The duke looked to his mother who simply shrugged her shoulders. He wondered if he could refute his sisters claims, telling her she was imagining it and that his hand had accidentally brushed against Rebecca's as they stood amongst the crowd of gathered servants. But she was far from stupid, so that was out of the question.

'You better not be dallying with her, Alex, she is my dearest friend. If you have done anything to hurt her, I shall never forgive you. I mean it.' Emma pointed a finger in his direction as she scolded him.

'I would never hurt her. I promise. You have my word.' He rose from his chair, suddenly having lost his appetite.

'So, you are going to walk away without explanation?' Emma cried after him.

'Emma, it is none of your business ... It is complicated,' Alex replied before exiting the room.

'I am furious with him, mother. He could likely have any woman of the ton, so why would he pick on Rebecca?'

'Why would he not? She is kind, funny, clever, and beautiful. I suspect he does not want to admit to himself that he is in love with her. Since he inherited the dukedom, he has tried to make everything perfect, even sacrificing love for duty.'

'You knew of his feelings for Rebecca, mother?'

'I suspected, I even hoped, as I think they are perfect for each other.' Evelyn placed an open hand over her heart. 'I wish for my children to have what I had with your father,' the dowager added tearfully, before reaching for a slice of toast.

Alexander slammed the front door of the house and walked out into the bright sunlight. He had decided to summon a carriage from the street rather that have his own readied for the journey he had planned. He had made a decision, and he needed to act on it right away.

CHAPTER SEVENTEEN

~~9♡℮~~

Rebecca was sitting on a bench in her sister's garden when Rosalind appeared at her side. As the ground floor of the house was a hive of activity, Rebecca had retreated to the garden for silence. Everyone was waiting on Robert hand and foot, his loud, angry voice constantly demanding brandy or laudanum.

'Rebecca, I am glad to have found you. We have much to discuss.' Rosalind fixed her skirts as she sat beside her younger sister on the stone bench.

'Do we?' Rebecca replied, deliberately wanting to sound curt

'Yes, of course we do. You are to be married soon, and due to Robert's accident, you will be staying here until the wedding.'

'I will *not* marry him, Rosalind. Robert cannot hurt or bully me while he lies in his bed,' Rebecca replied boldly.

'Do not be so stubborn, Rebecca. It is a good match for you. You will want for nothing. The gossip has yet to get out concerning Robert's gambling debt. The family name has still not been jeopardised, but we must act fast,' Rosalind countered.

'Rosalind, I do not care about the family name. Why does it concern you so?'

'No more questions now, *please,*' Rosalind was starting to get annoyed 'I will not discuss it further. What I wanted to say was that I have invited Lord Phillips to dine with us tomorrow evening, and I expect you to be on your best behaviour.'

Before Rebecca could react, her sister had gone, leaving her alone once more.

~

It was lunchtime when Alexander arrived at his destination, feeling nervous and excited about what he was going to do. Arriving at the estate he had been at not twenty-four hours previously; Alexander was ushered into the library to await Sir Thomas Redpath. He had also hoped to speak with his wife, Rose. As he waited, he crossed to the window that overlooked the gardens when he saw the familiar figure dressed in a floral day gown, her hair tied loosely at her nape. She did not fail to take his breath away every time he saw her. When Rebecca turned and he could see her more clearly, she looked utterly crestfallen.

'Your Grace, what do we owe to this honour? Twice in two days', Redpath asked in a friendly greeting, entering the library.

'Alexander, please. I cannot get used to these tedious titles. I was hoping to speak with yourself and your good lady,' he said as he fiddled with his pinkie ring. Alexander was becoming more aware of the nervous habit he had developed, playing with the piece of jewellery that had belonged to several dukes that came before him.

As if by magic, Rose entered to greet their guest out of courtesy, not expecting to join them, surprised when her husband asked her to take a seat due to the duke's request.

'What can we do for you?' Thomas was now standing next to the chair where his wife sat.

'I will not beat around the bush', Alexander smiled. 'I would like to offer for Lady Rebecca's hand in marriage.'

Although uncommonly nervous, the duke did not hesitate, far too excited by the prospect of Rebecca becoming his wife. He had decided to discuss his intentions with Rose and her husband due to the earl being indisposed. Although the right thing to do would be to speak with the elder sister, there was something about the viscountess that made him feel uneasy. All Rose could do was look at her husband to await his reaction, unprepared for what the duke had just said.

'You do know she is already promised to another, Alexander?' Thomas replied.

'Yes. I know of her brother's intentions to marry her off to Lord Phillips, and I also know how heartbroken Rebecca is at the prospect.'

Rose looked up to her husband with a smile. 'I think we need to call for Rebecca, as this very much involves her Thomas?'

~

Rebecca was still wandering the gardens when a maid came to inform her that her presence was required in the library. Surely Lord Phillips had not arrived early? No sounds were coming from the room; she had expected to hear his booming voice, but it all seemed unusually quiet. Nervously, she walked into the room. She was not prepared to see the Duke of Sandison staring back at her, her sister and brother-in-law gauging her reaction.

'Rebecca, sit down dear. His Grace wishes to speak with you.' Rose pointed to the chair opposite.

Rebecca bobbed a curtsy before taking a seat, instantly taken back to their encounter in this very room the night before, his vulgar language ringing in her ears and the memory of him devouring her with his mouth. She wondered if he was thinking the same.

'Do not look so worried, dear', her sister smiled, before looking at the duke, prompting him to speak.

Alexander crossed the room to where Rebecca sat. Leaning down, he took her hand, placing a light kiss on her bare knuckles, aware of her hastening breaths as he circled her wrist with his thumb. 'Lady Rebecca Rutherford, I have come here today to ask for your hand in marriage.'

'You want to *marry* me?' she practically shrieked, almost falling out of her chair.

'I want to marry you, yes.' Alexander felt slightly panicked all of a sudden, not so sure that she would agree to be his wife.

'You tease me, your Grace' she frowned.

'I do not, my Lady. I want to marry you. I will ask you again. Will you be my wife?'

Rebecca could not help bursting into a fit of giggles, a snort escaping as it had done like the day they had first met.

Her sister was now looking at her disapprovingly. 'Rebecca what on earth has come over you?'

'Sorry, I am so sorry. I am overwhelmed, that is all. You do realise I am not raised to be a duchess, your Grace,' Rebecca apologised.

'I am aware, but that no longer matters to me. It is you that I wish to make my wife and my duchess,' he replied.

If they had been alone, he would have taken her in his arms, before proving to her how much he wanted her to be his wife. Before his thoughts could become any more inappropriate, he was taken aback when Rebecca did something very un-duchess-like: she jumped from her chair and ran to Alexander, throwing her arms around him.

'Of course, I will marry you, Alex ... Even if you are one of the most infuriating people I have ever met.'

He kissed her on the lips, not caring that they were in polite company. But their reverie was interrupted by the sound of a woman gasping. Rosalind was standing at the open doorway, her face looking like thunder.

'What is going on in here?' she roared.

'I am to marry Alexander Fane, the Duke of Sandison, sister', Rebecca delighted in sharing this news as she held his hand tightly.

Rosalind laughed. 'Do *not* be ridiculous, Rebecca. You cannot be engaged when you are due to marry another.'

Rebecca looked Alexander in the eye while squeezing his hand. 'I am calling off the wedding, as of now.'

'You will do no such thing! A promise has been made and it will not be broken,' Rosalind screeched, her hands grasping the fabric of her dress.

Rosalind had not once directed the conversation to Alexander as she knew he was above her own social standing. He looked on, interested in what the eldest sister had to say.

Rebecca decided to ignore her sister's last remark and pulled Alexander by the hand that was still entwined with hers. 'Let us take a walk in the garden Alex, *my lov*e.' She knew it was childish when she poked her tongue out while pushing past her stuck-up sister, but she did it anyway.

~

Walking arm-in-arm further out into the grounds of the vast estate, Rebecca turned to Alexander. 'You did not have to ask me to marry you, Alex. I wanted you to do those things to me.'

'Is that why you think I asked?'

'Why else would you ask someone like me to marry you? You are a Duke, and I am the youngest child of an earl. I am also brazen and audacious, according to many', she grinned.

'Rebecca, I have grown to care for you a great deal. Brazen and audacious are just two of the many things that I love about you.'

'Love?', Rebecca gasped.

Alexander checked to see how far they were from the main house, desperate to scoop her into his arms and carry her off somewhere private. Spinning her to face him, he playfully squeezed her rump as he nibbled her ear.

'How could I not, Rebecca?' he said, raising his hand to stroke her cheek.

Turning her head, she kissed the hand that caressed her face. 'I am glad as I love you too'.

They stood for a moment, looking at each other in silence, before Rebecca spoke. 'There is an unused cottage just over the hill,' she announced breathily.

'Is there really? And why do you tell me this? he teased, making her blush.

Taking a deep breath, she decided to play him at his own game. 'Because I am aching for you Alex, I need more. I need you inside me.'

Not believing the sinful words that had left Rebecca's lips, he was instantly aroused. 'Show me the way now!' he ordered, grabbing her hand tightly and pulling her until they were both running in the direction of the cottage.

The old gamekeeper's cottage sat within a little overgrown garden that had been badly neglected over time. When they pushed open the slightly rotting wooden door, it was a pleasant surprise to see that the inside was not as disregarded as the outside, with sheets draped over the small amount of furniture that remained.

Unable to wait any longer, Alexander lifted Rebecca off the floor so she could wrap her legs around him, her head thrown back giving him access to kiss her slender neck.

'I do not know how long I can wait to take you as my wife', he growled into her neck.

'I am sure you have certain privileges as a duke for things to move quickly, your Grace,' she said cheekily, knowing how he hated it when she used his title.

Giving her bottom a light spank in retaliation, he placed Rebecca back on her feet, turning her so he could unbutton her gown. It was all happening so quickly that Rebecca had scarcely noticed the remainder of her clothing being removed as she now stood only in her silk stockings. Alexander did not take his eyes from her naked form as he sat on the small bed removing his boots, beckoning her to come closer when he had finally removed his trousers.

Rebecca stood between his naked legs so he could take a pert nipple in his mouth, sucking and licking the hard bud, repeating the action on the other one before running his tongue over her soft belly and naval.

'Alex, I will not be able to stand upright for much longer if you continue to do that,' she said breathlessly.

'We must remedy that immediately, then.' He responded by pinning her down on the mattress, rubbing his hard cock against her wet folds.

'Fuck, you are soaking wet,' he cursed.

Alexander groaned with desire as he made his way down her body with licks and kisses, sucking hard on her fleshy breast, not caring that he would leave a mark; she was his now. Taking delight in the feel of her silk stockings against his bare skin, he ran his hands up her legs, spreading her wider to his gaze before burying his head between her thighs.

'You can make as much noise as you wish while I feed on your pretty little cunny. No one will hear you', he growled while nibbling on soft flesh before kissing the damp curls between her thighs.

Rebecca purred when she felt his first lick, but when he buried his tongue deeper, she could not stop herself from crying out. Every flick of his tongue made her want more. Alexander ran his hand up her thigh as his tongue continued to massage her wet folds, her hands now pulling at his hair as she thrust herself towards him. Rebecca almost screamed when he inserted a finger next to where his tongue was circling her hardened nub.

'Alex. I need you to make love to me. I need more. I need all of you,' she begged.

Slowly removing his mouth from between her legs and sliding back up the small bed, Alexander positioned himself until he hovered over her.

'Are you sure this is what you want, Rebecca?'

'Yes, I am sure. I need you,' she pleaded.

Rebecca had heard that it could be painful the first time, but she trusted him wholeheartedly. Alexander placed tender kisses over Rebecca's face and neck before they joined mouths, the kissing becoming more heated and passionate. Distracting her from the initial discomfort she would feel, Alex held her tightly as she gasped when he first entered her, but the pain did not last long. She was soon experiencing a different sensation as he stretched her, the feeling of fullness and pleasure was overwhelming. His first groan of ecstasy sent shivers throughout her body.

'I need to move inside you now, but I will stop if it pains you,' he soothed.

'Please, Alex. I need you to teach me everything.'

When he started to move, Rebecca instinctively wrapped her legs around his waist, allowing him to thrust deeper. He cursed and groaned as his movements became faster. Rebecca could feel herself climaxing again, allowing herself to scream his name this time, and it was not long before she felt Alexander's body tighten as he shouted out with his own release.

Lying side-by-side in the small bed, Alexander twisted her hair between his fingers as she lazily watched him. He had never felt so satisfied, although he was slightly embarrassed with himself for spending so quickly. But the effect she had on him, especially when she screamed his name, had made him lose all self-control. He had not even had time to withdraw before spilling his seed inside her, which was something he never did.

'I wish we could stay like this forever,' Rebecca said as she tried to stay awake.

'Soon, my love', Alexander replied, kissing her gently on the lips, excited for their future as husband and wife, and having her lying in his arms like this every day.

CHAPTER EIGHTEEN

Alexander was humming a tune to himself as he perused the books in his library. Having had just experienced the most thrilling afternoon of his life, he was now fantasising about all the ways that he would pleasure Rebecca when they were wed. He had not yet told his mother and sister that he was to be married but was sure they would be happy for him, if not a little shocked.

'Alex, what is that dreadful noise you are making?' Emma had been passing when she had heard him singing and humming to himself, surprised by his cheerfulness.

'Is mother about? I have something quite urgent that we must discuss', he asked, purposefully ignoring her jibe.

~

Rebecca was happier than she had been in her entire life; she was hopelessly in love with Alexander Fane and she was sure that he felt the same way. She was unable to think of anything else but her future as the duke's wife and the family that they would have. It had slipped her mind that Rosalind had invited Lord Phillips to dine with them this evening. Her mood soured slightly when she reached the bottom of the staircase, recognising Lord Phillip's voice emanating from the room that had been made up for her brother while he recuperated. There was also another much quieter voice, which she soon recognised was her sister, Rosalind.

'I promise you that I have spoken with her, my Lord. She is aware that you will be married in two weeks, hence. Do not fret, *please*.' Rosalind spoke quietly so any passing servant would not hear.

'The chit better be standing at that alter or I will inform everyone about your brother's unsavoury habits and how he tried to sell his sister to me in payment of his debt. His *own* sister. Can you imagine the scandal?' Phillips threatened.

There was a short silence before he spoke again. 'It also appears that I may be able to add his latest addiction to the list.' The Lord was implying that the earl was going to become reliant on the laudanum that he was currently taking for his pain. 'I need a wife that will not only provide me with an heir but gain me acceptance within the ton. I want my name to be acknowledged and respected,' he bellowed.

Rebecca listened at the door, jumping at the sound of fists hitting wood when Lord Phillips had spoken of being acknowledged and respected, appearing obsessed with the notion.

While she continued listening at the door, Rosalind spoke next. 'Please keep your voice down, my Lord. Can you not see that my brother is sleeping? He is not well.'

'He is well enough, Viscountess. He sleeps because of the opium. The room reeks of it.'

There were a few more exchanges between the pair before the movement in the room suggested they were about to leave, forcing Rebecca to step away from her eavesdropping.

~

'Mother, please stop crying.' Alexander was removing a handkerchief from his jacket pocket, ready to hand it to the dowager duchess.

'I cannot help it, Alexander, I am so happy. I could never have imagined that you would marry for love,' Evelyn sniffed. 'Is it not the most wonderful news, Emma?'

Not having said a word, Emma sat tapping her fingers on the arm of the chair, eyeing her brother dubiously. 'Did you *compromise* her? Is she with child? She is, she *is* with child, you are a brute, Alexander Fane. How could you?' Emma ranted.

'Lady Emma Fane, that is a dreadful thing to say. Apologise to your brother immediately,' Evelyn scolded.

Emma did so reluctantly. Alexander persisted. 'No, of course I did not compromise her, Emma. Why do you find it so hard to believe that we have fallen in love?'

'You do not even *like* each other. I refuse to believe you.' Emma stood up, turned on her heels and left the room.

Alexander sat beside his mother on the chaise. The dowager had now stopped snivelling, taking his hand in hers, a slight look of worry etched on her face. The conversation suddenly became serious as Evelyn asked him about Rebecca's betrothal to Lord Phillips and whether her brother knew she was breaking off the engagement.

'We have decided it best that we tell him together. I do not think it is safe for Rebecca to do so on her own.' Although Rebecca's brother was currently incapacitated, there was no knowing what Lord Phillips might do when he heard of it. There was also something about her eldest sister that he did not trust.

~

Sitting at the dinner table with her family had always felt like a chore due to Rosalind criticising Rebecca's every move, whether it be the way she was sitting or how she held her cutlery. This evening was no exception, especially as Lord Phillips dined with them, still under the illusion that he was marrying her. Thankfully, Rose and Sir Thomas were at the table which meant that the conversation was not solely about the upcoming wedding.

'You look especially lovely this evening, my Lady', Phillips leered at Rebecca as he complimented her. 'You will make the most alluring bride.'

'Thank you, my Lord,' she answered, disgusted at how he slurped his soup and spoke with his mouth full, never mind that he used the word *alluring* when describing her.

Well, I am never going to be your bride, so there.

The meal seemed to go on forever, Phillips prattling on about himself and his achievements in business and the wonderful life she was going to have. Rosalind nodded her head in agreement, occasionally looking over to Rebecca.

If he mentions the wedding one more time, I am going to have to say something.

Rebecca had noticed that her sister Rose was very quiet throughout the meal, at times squirming when Lord Phillips spoke. Rebecca desperately wanted Rose or Sir Thomas to mention Alexander's proposal and that the wedding was to be called off, but they had told her it would not be discussed over the impromptu dinner Rosalind had organised as they had things to consider regarding what his reaction might be.

Rosalind, on the other hand, had made up her mind that Rebecca would still be marrying Phillips, refusing to acknowledge the duke's proposal, carrying on as if nothing was amiss.

Once the meal was finished, it was suggested that they retire to the drawing room. Sir Thomas had excused himself due to urgent business commitments, although Rebecca suspected he did not wish to spend any more time in the company of Lord Phillips. The ladies had some respite from the man when he excused himself to use the water closet.

'I am *not* marrying him.' The words had left Rebecca's mouth before she could even think of the consequences.

'What on earth are you talking about?' Rosalind hissed through her teeth. 'Of course, you are marrying him, Rebecca. Enough of this *Duke* nonsense. It has to *stop*!'

Rebecca held her head high, determined not to be dominated by her sister. 'I am not marrying him; I *will* marry Alexander.'

Rebecca thought Rosalind was going to explode. Her face turning a dark shade of pink, she gripped the arm of the chair until her knuckles whitened.

'You will *not* embarrass me or this family, Rebecca Rutherford. I will not allow it.' The viscountess was trying not to raise her voice, fearing that Lord Phillips would hear.

'If you cared about this family, you would never allow your sister to marry such a vile man,' Rebecca replied before storming from the room.

Phillips appeared at the parlour door, confused as to why it was only Rosalind who greeted him. The viscountess quickly informed him that Lady Rebecca had retired to her chambers due to a headache, although the look on Phillips' face suggested he did not believe a word of it.

Rebecca was sitting at the top of the staircase waiting for the lord to leave, conscious that the conversation with Rosalind was far from over. She glanced to the foot of the stairs, remembering the sight of her brother lying at the bottom, feeling no sympathy for the man who had bullied her for her whole life.

Satisfied that Phillips was on his way, Rebecca stood up, ready to head to her chamber when she saw that Rosalind was furiously marching towards her, lifting her skirts as she ascended the stairs.

Here we go, the wicked sister is not happy.

Moving slightly faster than was considered ladylike, Rebecca continued along the hallway rather than wait for her sister to berate her.

'Rebecca! You will *stop*, right now', her sister snarled.

Reaching the door to her room, Rebecca turned to face her sister who was now seething, 'I have nothing to say that I have not said already, Rosalind. Good night.'

The viscountess ignored her younger sister, entering the room behind her, slamming the door so hard that the trinkets on Rebecca's dressing table rattled.

'Rosalind, you cannot just come in. This is my private room. Please, will you just leave me alone,' Rebecca yelled, not caring who heard.

'Do you have more secrets to hide other than your betrothal to the Duke of Sandison and the rags that you hide under the mattress?'

'Rags? What do you mean rags?' Rebecca replied, confused.

'Do not act *stupid*. The clothing that you plan to run away in. Did you think that you could fool me, you stupid girl? It is the oldest trick in the book, disguising oneself as a maid to escape unnoticed!'

Rebecca was not upset at Rosalind taking the clothes, but she was devastated that her own sister would go through her private things.

'Did you not think a maid would discover them when changing your bedsheets? Luckily, I overheard the girls talking or you just might have got away with it,' the viscountess sneered.

'Get out Rosalind. I do not wish to talk to you, and I do not care one jot that you discovered the clothing because I do not need to run now that I am no longer marrying Lord Phillips'.

CHAPTER NINETEEN

Alexander was sitting in his club discussing business with Benjamin when he saw his friend looking at him strangely. 'There is something different about you, Alex, but I cannot think what it is.' Benjamin stroked his chin as he continued to peer at Alex quizzically.

'Is there?' he replied.

'I suspect it may have something to do with a certain young lady,' Benjamin smirked.

'Perhaps,' the duke grinned.

'Lady Rebecca Rutherford *perhaps*. For God's sake, Fane the suspense is killing me.'

Alexander was becoming quite amused at his friend's questioning, considering whether to drag things out a little longer. Alexander would normally have taken pleasure tormenting the young viscount, but he could not contain himself much longer, wanting to announce his engagement to Rebecca from the rooftops.

'I am to be married,' The duke announced proudly, leaning forward in his chair so as not to be overheard by the other patrons.

Alexander and never known his friend to be lost for words, although it did not last long.

'Well, well, well. The duke has chosen his duchess, and a fine choice she is my friend, although I was sure you were going to choose a lady that was not so, how shall I say *spirited*.'

Benjamin raised his glass in a toast before summoning a waiter to bring refills. The night continued in the same manner, the drink flowing and the men's chatter getting louder and more boisterous.

'Lady Rebecca Rutherford is the kindest, funniest, most beautiful creature that I have ever met, and I cannot wait to make her my duchess,' Alexander slurred a little to loudly, almost falling off his chair while Benjamin laughed heartily.

'You may mock me, Turner, but Cupid will hit you with his little arrow one day.'

'I would not be averse to that, Fane. I would also be happy with a marriage of convenience if she has a pleasant countenance and ample breasts,' the viscount sniggered, winking at his friend.

'You are a rogue, Turner. I look forward to the day that you are captivated by a lady who will not put up with your rakish ways.'

'I drink to that, my old chum, I drink to that... Slan-cha-va, my friend. Good Health.'

'Slainte Mhaath,' Alexander replied.

~

The following morning, not long after the family had finished breakfast, the silence of the household was interrupted by frantic banging on the front door. When the elderly butler accompanied by a much younger member of the household opened the door, they were greeted by a red-faced Lord Phillips, demanding they give him entry and an audience with Robert Rutherford. Rosalind appeared from a room down the hall, a knowing look on her worried face as Phillips continued ranting, insisting that he speak to the earl.

'My brother is unable to accept visitors today as he is quite unwell', the viscountess informed him, guiding him away from where the servants stood watching the drama unfold. When Phillips realised he would not be able to speak to the earl, he insisted on speaking to Sir Thomas; although he, too, was not at home.

'I shall await his return', he replied angrily, striding down the hallway towards the parlour that he had been entertained in previously, as if he could do whatever he wished. Rosalind closely followed at his back, suspecting the reason for his impromptu visit to her sister's residence. Rosalind herself was only supposed to be staying with Rose until after the birth of her nephew, but due to her brother's accident she had stayed on to oversee his care. Lord Phillips paced back and forth, muttering obscenities as Rosalind sat herself in one of the larger armchairs, her hands resting on her lap, nervously clasping and unclasping her fingers.

'What the hell is going on?' he suddenly roared.

Flinching at the sudden outburst and annoyed at how she had been spoken to, Rosalind sat herself up straighter in the chair, looking the furious lord in the eye.

'How dare you speak to me in such a way. If you cannot speak to me kindly, I must ask you to leave.'

'Ha, it is not your home, viscountess, so I will not leave, unless the master or mistress of the house asks me to do so.'

'If my husband was to witness the way you disrespect me, he would have you banished from every establishment in the country that you frequent', she spat back.

'Your *husband*. Where is he? Is he here or is he also out? I would rather speak to him than his *woman.*' His lip curling, he looked around, as if the viscount were hiding somewhere in the room.

Rosalind had not kept her husband updated on the betrothal between her youngest sister and the lord as he was a busy man who had little interest in his wife's private affairs. She now regretted not informing him, as the man standing in front of her was becoming more and more threatening in his behaviour. Maybe if she had not been so obsessed with her reputation, Rosalind would have asked Malcolm to investigate Phillip's character further before welcoming him into the family. If her husband were to observe this current behaviour from the lord, he would have him on the first ship to the Colonies after a good beating.

'Whether you like it or not, there are no gentlemen home other than my brother, *and* as I said, he is *not* accepting visitors', she replied stoically.

'Lady Rebecca Rutherford, my betrothed, where is she? Is she in or is she out too, whoring herself to Sandison?' he roared.

~

Rebecca was returning from a morning stroll around the garden, more furious at her sister than she had been the night before. She had no right to go through her private belongings, so Rebecca planned on confronting Rosalind again this morning. They needed to sit down and talk about this whole mess of a situation. This was all entirely her brother's fault, yet he now lay incapacitated, full of laudanum, unable to walk or make any rational decisions; leaving others to clear up *his* mess.

Since staying at Rose's, she had overheard some conversations between Rose and her husband regarding her brother. It was clear that Rose was trying to find the good in her sibling, but her husband did not speak of him so kindly. Language such as entitled, debauched lifestyle, and addicted were often used when Sir Thomas had been discussing Robert Rutherford. He had even mentioned Rosalind's name on occasion, but Rebecca had been unable to hear that chat clearly.

As soon as Rebecca stepped into the entrance to the house, she was aware that something was going on, and was surprised to see two of the servants standing outside the closed door to the parlour as if eavesdropping. When they saw Rebecca, the maids scurried off in the opposite direction, looking embarrassed to have been caught listening at the door.

~

Alexander was up, washed and dressed earlier than usual, keen to visit Lady Rebecca so they could discuss their betrothal with her family. He was unaware that she had already told her eldest sister, and it had not gone down well at all. Alexander had planned on having a light breakfast before travelling to the Redpath's residence but was suddenly unable to stomach even a mere morsel of food, he was so keen to be on his way. Summoning his carriage, he would leave right away.

Rosalind had not expected Phillips to speak of her sister in such demeaning terms, finding that she did not like how he spoke of her youngest sibling. 'You do *not* speak of my sister in such a way. You will leave now, or I will summon a footman to remove you.'

'I speak of her as the harlot that she is, and she *will* marry me. She will *never* marry that bastard Sandison', he snarled.

'What do you mean, marry the duke?' Rosalind tried to sound convincing as she knew fine well that her sister had a desire to marry Sandison.

'Do not lie to me, viscountess. I had to hear it from an associate that had been at Whites and witnessed a drunken conversation between Fane and his friend,' he bellowed.

There was nothing Rosalind could say that would calm the lord's anger. She knew she had to get him out of the house and consider what should be done next.

'I am sorry that you had to hear such a thing from your associate. Is it not possible that it may be an untruth, my lord?' she said while trying to placate him.

'For your sake and that of your brother's, it had better *not* be the truth.'

Rosalind got up from her chair, hopeful that it would encourage Phillips to leave but it did not have the desired effect. He remained where he stood. Thinking quickly, she suggested checking to see if her brother was awake and lucid enough to receive him, although highly unlikely. She did not wish to be alone in his company any longer as his mood and mannerisms were becoming more enraged and erratic. Pouring the lord a large brandy, Rosalind excused herself to check on her brother, advising him that she would not be long and that a servant would bring him to the earl shortly.

~

Rebecca had heard voices from inside the parlour but did not want to enter as it was not her home; whatever interested the servants should not really concern her. Deciding to go to her room and collect the latest gothic novel that Flora had smuggled in, she would head to the drawing room and relax for a while before confronting her eldest sibling.

Settling herself in a plush armchair, Rebecca opened her book to the first chapter, hoping to lose herself in the story that she would be discussing with her friends when they next met, something that she had greatly missed due to recent events. Sitting with her back to the door, it took Rebecca a minute to realise that someone had entered the room. Assuming that it was one of her sisters, she continued to finish the page she was already engrossed in before looking up.

'Rebecca, Rebecca. What a coincidence to find you here,' Phillips hissed as he crossed the room after closing the door.

Surprised at his sudden appearance, Rebecca was unable to speak as she watched the odious man stride towards her, his face contorted with rage.

'Nothing to say to me, my lady, mmm?' he sneered, leaning into her with his meaty hands gripping the arms of her chair.

Rebecca could smell the fresh brandy radiating from him the closer he got, pushing at his chest she finally found her voice. 'Kindly remove yourself, Lord Phillips.'

'Or *what*? Your dashing duke is not here to save you now, my dear,' he licked his lips while looking her up and down.

Rebecca felt real fear for the first time in her life but wanted to remain calm so continued to push at his chest as his fleshy fingers grasped the chair tighter. Unable to push him away, his body towering over her, she felt his leg press into her forcing her legs apart so that he could position himself between her skirts. When her dress began to ride up Rebecca knew that she could not allow him to cage her in, the look on his face becoming more sinister.

Feeling disgusted when she saw the obvious outline of his manhood, she was reminded of a book that she had read that detailed a similar attack. Curling her petite hand into a fist she drew it back before punching him as hard as she could between his legs. Watching as he stumbled backwards with a howl, Rebecca took the opportunity to jump from her chair, putting some distance between them.

'You little whore, you will pay for that!' he cried, obviously in some pain.

'I do not fear you, my Lord. You are nothing but a bully and a weasel. I will never be yours ... *never*.'

Rebecca cautiously moved towards the closed door while Phillips tried to catch his breath. She was just about to reach for the doorknob when a sweaty hand sunk into her shoulder, pulling at the fabric of her dress, causing it to rip.

'You will not defy me. *No one* defies me. Especially not a woman who opens her legs for any man that looks her way,' he threatened.

'How dare you', she said, feeling his spittle on the now bare skin of her shoulder as he roared at her, inwardly praying that someone would come to her rescue soon.

The next thing Rebecca felt was the wall as he pushed her hard against it, both his hands ripping at her gown to expose more of her arms and shoulders. She screamed as she thrashed her body trying to free herself of his clutches.

'Do not struggle so much, you will enjoy me more than *him*', he whispered in her ear.

'Get off me, please', she begged as she felt his manhood against her backside and his hands on her waist. Pressed against the wall with her eyes tightly shut, Rebecca started to count in her head hoping that the attack would be over as soon as possible.

~

Alexander was on his way to see the woman who he now knew he was madly in love with. He did not hold a bouquet of flowers or a sweet treat but a book that he knew she would cherish. Running his thumb over the leather cover, he smiled as he recalled the time he first set eyes on the bold beautiful woman who was to be his wife, watching the passing scenery from the carriage window unable to imagine a future without her in it.

~

Rebecca did not realise that someone else was now in the room. She had disconnected herself from the assault, not even noticing that Lord Phillips's hands and lips were no longer on her person. Slowly turning, Rebecca watched as her sister Rosalind stood over the lifeless body that now lay on the floor, blood escaping a wound to the head. A single tear running down her pale face. The viscountess held a bloodied candlestick tightly in her hand.

Everything started to move quickly, the butler and several other servants dashed into the room, the elderly housekeeper guiding Rosalind to the sofa, prising the candlestick from her fingers. Rebecca was now on her knees staring at the lifeless body of Lord Phillips.

'My lady, you must step away now. Come sit, the butler said gently.

Rebecca allowed the butler to help her up, while she pulled at the torn fabric of her gown to cover herself.

~

When Alexander's carriage pulled up and he climbed out, he was greeted by the sight of Rose talking to a man wearing a familiar blue uniform. The duke suddenly had a nervous feeling in his gut, aware that something serious had happened due to the sight of the constable. Taking a deep breath, he walked to where Rose was standing. Hearing the approaching footsteps, she looked up at him before bursting into tears. Alexander instantly panicked, waiting for Rose to say something, not able to bring himself to ask what was going on. Rose had noticed the distressed look on Alexander's face, stepping closer before placing a gentle, reassuring hand on his forearm.

'She is safe now, she is fine', Rose smiled through her tears.

Alexander turned and ran up the front steps of the house. Similar to when Robert Rutherford had fallen down the stairs, the hall was in chaos; several constables were speaking to servants and Dr Fleming was closing his medical bag as he spoke with Sir Thomas.

Rebecca was clutching the woollen blanket that was draped over her shoulders to protect her modesty as she had not yet been able to change her gown, waiting to be questioned by the local constable. Sitting in the drawing room, her head bowed, afraid to look up when she heard the door open. Even though she knew Phillips was dead, she still flinched with the memory of what had happened earlier.

'Rebecca, my love', Alexander said gently as he knelt in front of her. 'It is *me* … Please look at me … What has happened?'

Rebecca threw herself into his arms and sobbed while he held her tight, never wanting to let her go. As he wrapped his arms around her the blanket fell from her shoulders revealing her torn gown.

'Oh God, Rebecca. What did they do to you? Please tell me!'

'Lord Phillips, he tried to …' Unable to finish her sentence, she burst into tears again.

Alexander sat back, taking her face in his hands, while using his thumb to wipe away a tear.

'I will kill the bastard. I will bloody *kill* him,' he raged.

Rebecca shook her head, taking his hands from her face, and holding them tightly.

'He is already dead, Alex. Rosalind killed him.'

Alexander reluctantly left Rebecca with Rose so he could speak to Sir Thomas. Rebecca was in no state to relay what had happened and he needed to know what had taken place.

A tall imposing gentleman with sandy coloured hair that was greying at the temples had joined the conversation between the doctor and Sir Thomas. When Thomas saw Alexander, he motioned for him to join them. Alexander was introduced to the man previously unknown to him as Rosalind's husband, Viscount Lanton.

'What the hell has happened, Redpath? Rebecca said that Phillips is dead', Alexander probed.

Sir Thomas looked at the viscount as if wanting permission to answer, but it was Lanton who spoke.

'Sadly, it is true. Lord Phillips died earlier due to a severe blow to his head. It is believed that he was attacking Lady Rebecca. My wife heard...'

'*Your* wife?' Alexander interrupted Lanton as he began to explain.

'The viscountess was the one that struck him. She had walked into the room while he was assaulting Lady Rebecca', Lanton answered.

The two men continued to explain what they knew of the incident to the Alexander, and that because the constables believed the attack was in self-defence, it was unlikely that any charges would be brought against Rosalind. But they would need to speak to Rebecca. Alexander had seen how upset she was, so insisted that he sat with her throughout the questioning by the police.

Rebecca held Alexander's hand as she told them how Phillips pushed her against the wall, ripping her dress. She told of how he had touched her body and kissed her neck before Rosalind had hit him over the head to make him stop. Alexander sat quietly, occasionally squeezing her hand while encouraging her to tell the constables everything she could.

Judging by his demeanour as Rebecca recounted what he had done, Alexander would have likely killed the man if he was not already dead. There were moments when she cried and other moments when she was plain angry. Rebecca knew that she would get through it because Alexander was by her side.

When her questioning was over, Rebecca and Alexander escaped the chaos of the house by stepping outside for some time alone. They walked hand-in-hand through the garden, stopping occasionally to share a kiss while using all their restraint not to lie down on the grass and make love. Wrapping his arms around her Alexander gazed into her green eyes as he mouthed, *I love you.*

'I love you too, Alex ... More than you will ever know.' Smiling, Rebecca stood on her tiptoes and kissed him softly on the lips.

'Would two weeks be too soon to marry, my love?' he asked nervously as he already held the special licence in his pocket.

'Not soon enough, *your Grace*', she teased.

Alexander lifted Rebecca off the ground, spinning her around as she shrieked for him to put her down. He had worried what her reaction might be when he mentioned their wedding due to what had happened earlier, but she was as elated as he was, eager to be his Duchess. Her tears from earlier having dried, she wore a fresh gown and her whole face lit up with her wide smile, delighting Alexander when her little tooth gap was visible. Rebecca did not want Phillips to win; yes, he was dead, but she would never allow the memory of his horrendous actions to destroy her happiness with her duke.

CHAPTER TWENTY

T hat was quite a frightening tale, Felicity', Katherine said.
Emma opened the curtains to let in the daylight. It had been several weeks since the friends had all been together. 'You read it beautifully. I could feel the hairs on the back of my neck stand up.'

'I do hope that we can continue to meet like this when you are married, Rebecca', Felicity fretted, 'We have so many stories to read.'

'I still cannot believe you want to marry my brother,' Emma joked.

Rebecca never imagined she could be so happy, surrounded by her friends, laughing and joking, knowing the man she loved would be her husband the following week.

'Well, you *must* believe it, as I will soon be your sister,' she replied.

The good friends continued to discuss the book that they had been reading, along with some gossip about people they knew. Now that all the ladies were engrossed in conversation, Rebecca thought she could quietly slip out of the room. It did not go unnoticed as Emma's eyes followed her suspiciously.

'Where are you off to in such a hurry?'

The first excuse that Rebecca could think of was that she needed to use the water closet, sure that no one would question it. 'I believe I have had too many cups of tea. If you will excuse me for a moment.'

Alexander was sitting at his desk without his jacket or waistcoat, his shirtsleeves rolled up to the elbow while he studied the ledgers in front of him. He had found it hard to concentrate, knowing that Rebecca was in a room only a few doors away from where he worked, counting down the days until she would be living with him in this very house. As if he had willed her to appear, Rebecca glided into the room, a huge smile on her face, dressed in a pale blue dress with a matching ribbon woven through her hair. Alexander could still not quite believe that someone as beautiful as Rebecca wanted to marry him.

'Come here, right now', he demanded, beckoning her to come sit on his lap by slapping his thigh.

'I do not have much time, but I needed to see you', Rebecca purred as he began to stroke his hands up her legs while kissing her neck, the now familiar scent of lavender drawing her in.

'Is the door locked?' he asked.

When she nodded, Alexander proceeded to undo his trousers, releasing himself while Rebecca pushed up her gown to give him access to her aching core. Running the tip of his finger along her slit, he groaned when he felt how wet she was.

'Do you want to ride me? You are so beautifully wet. Are you wet just for me, my love?'

'Yes, oh yes, I am so wet... Just for you,' she whispered seductively.

Alexander took his large cock and rubbed it up and down her wet folds before positioning Rebecca on his lap so he could insert himself fully. He almost instantly became undone when she let out a long sigh as he guided her up and down on his swollen length. It did not take her long to find a rhythm that gave intense pleasure to them both. They devoured each other's mouths, their tongues tangling as they groaned with desire for each other. It was not long before they were both spent, Rebecca staying on his lap, her forehead pressed against him while he stroked her bare bottom beneath her dress.

'I must go back now before Emma comes looking for me. She was definitely suspicious when I left.'

Alexander watched Rebecca as she walked away, laughing out loud when she exaggerated the sway of her hips, aware of his eyes on her.

~

As Rebecca was being primped and preened by no less than three maids, there was a gentle knock on the door before it burst open with gusto, allowing Emma, Matilda, Felicity, and Katherine to bounce in. The four young ladies held hands while admiring their friend.

'Oh, Rebecca, you have never looked more beautiful,' Katherine sniffed.

'I cannot believe that after today we shall be sisters.' Emma could not contain the excitement she felt. Initially untrusting of her brother's intentions towards Rebecca, she now saw how deep their love was for each other. 'And a duchess at that,' she added.

'Is that not the most amusing thing that you have ever heard?' Rebecca giggled. '*Me*, a duchess.'

The friends all agreed that it was indeed amusing that Rebecca would soon be the Duchess of Sandison, reminding her of the more mischievous antics she had partaken in over the years, and how it was imperative that she must now behave in a *completely respectable manner*.

Rebecca scoffed at the very thought of respectability. If she had been respectable, she would not be marrying Alex this morning. It was her brazenness that captured his attention in the first place.

~

'Mother, you must stop crying. You do not want to welcome guests with red eyes and a running nose', Alexander shook his head as he passed the dowager duchess his handkerchief.

'Oh, Alexander. I just wish your father was here to see this day. To see his son marrying for love, and to Rebecca Rutherford at that,' she sniffled into the handkerchief. 'He was quite fond of the girl, you know.'

'Yes, I know he was mother, and she of him.'

Crossing the room to comfort his mother who sat on the small sofa, he placed a hand on her shoulder. Alexander felt a lump forming in his throat when he remembered his father but was glad that the late duke had met Rebecca and thought of her fondly. Mother and son chatted for a while longer about his father and how proud he was of his children before Evelyn suddenly announced that it was time to leave for the church, smoothing down her gown as she got to her feet. She had been in mourning colours since losing her beloved husband, but today she wore a dark green that complimented her ageless skin.

'Mother, you look beautiful,' he remarked, quickly regretting his words when she began to cry again.

Rose was standing at the doorway, watching her youngest sister laughing and joking with her dearest friends, looking radiant in a white gown of silk and lace. Her chestnut hair cascaded down her back in soft curls adorned with bejewelled pins. Over the last few months, the sisters had become much closer, enjoying spending time together, finding that they had more in common than they would ever have thought, including a love for the same dark novels.

Rebecca had been living with Rose and Sir Thomas while Robert Rutherford continued to recover; he had returned to live at his own residence under the care of physicians paid for by Sir Thomas. As well as his physical injuries from the fall, he was being treated for alcohol and opium addictions which had become quite worrisome. Rebecca had not visited the earl and had no plans to do so, unable to forgive him for the way he had treated her over the years.

Noticing her sister from across the room, Rebecca gestured with her hands for her sister to join them in the final preparations before she left for the church, another visitor arriving at her back.

'Can I come in?' Flora asked, having to speak louder than normal to be heard over the gossiping.

'Flora.' standing up as a maid tried to put the finishing touches to her hair, Rebecca opened her arms to embrace the woman who she considered a close friend. Flora would soon be leaving her service as she too was soon to be married, much to Rebecca's delight.

'Flora, you look wonderful. The colour of your dress is beautiful.'

Rebecca had wanted Flora to attend her wedding as a guest, insisting that she treat her to a new gown for the occasion as a thank-you for her friendship and kindness over the years. 'Is George with you?'

Blushing slightly at the mention of her betrothed, Flora said he would be joining her at the church later, before accepting a glass of champagne from Lady Matilda.

~

Standing on the steps of the small parish church, Benjamin Turner at his side, Alexander wore a dark blue frock coat, complimented by a sharp white waistcoat that he tugged on nervously. Neither Rebecca nor Alexander had wanted a big society wedding; they had favoured a smaller more intimate setting with the one's dearest to them.

Benjamin puffed on a cigar, in between joking with his friend that he still had time to call off the wedding, earning him a playful punch in the arm from the duke. Removing a small flask from his frockcoat pocket that contained the finest Scottish Whisky, Alexander took a slug before offering the flask to the viscount.

'Nervous, old boy?'Benjamin teased as he stubbed out his cigar and took a drink, exaggerating when he swallowed that the liquid burned his throat. 'You can still run you know,' he japed when he recognised the carriage coming over the hill.

Alexander just looked at him in despair and took another swig of whisky.

'Could this be your beloved arriving now?' Benjamin said, slapping the duke on the back.

This was Alexander's signal to make his way into the church. Benjamin followed, taking his seat in the front pew alongside the dowager duchess, who dabbed her eyes with a handkerchief as she proudly watched her son.

Felicity, Katherine, and Matilda stepped out of the first carriage, each one wearing a different shade of blue, ready to escort Rebecca into the church, Emma had accompanied the bride in the carriage that followed closely behind.

Alexander stood facing the altar when he sensed Rebecca was entering the church. Turning, he was greeted by the sight of her closest friends ready to take their seats, each one a vision in blue. Emma smiled and nodded to him in approval. Rebecca waited for her friends to take their seats before she began her slow walk down the aisle.

Alexander felt a lump form in his throat as Lady Rebecca Rutherford walked towards him. She was breathtakingly beautiful and gave him the widest smile as he winked at her playfully. Rebecca had wanted to run down the aisle into his arms when she saw him standing alone. He looked anxious as he fidgeted with the ring on his little finger, which he only did, she noticed when he was nervous. Which was very rare.

He mouthed to her how beautiful she looked when she reached his side, and she responded by mouthing *I love you*.

The vicar looked at the couple that now faced him as he began to speak in his deep, dry-sounding voice, 'Dearly beloved. *We are gathered together here in the sight of God* ...'

Rebecca was barely listening to the elderly gentleman who was poised in front of her, impatient for the service to be over so she could begin her new life as Alexander's wife. As they repeated their vows in front of the people most precious to them, the only other sound was that of quiet sobbing from the front pew.

After what felt like forever, the vicar pronounced that they were man and wife. Alexander took his new Duchess by the waist, pulling her into his arms. Going against all propriety, he kissed her passionately on the lips, not caring that he had the eyes of the congregation on him. She returned the kiss with the same vigour.

'Highly inappropriate, your Graces', Benjamin jested from where he sat, which caused a bout of laughter from the small congregation and a disapproving look from Lady Emma Fane.

Everyone was invited back to the duke and duchess's residence to enjoy a feast fit for Kings. Alexander watched his new duchess as she welcomed everyone with open arms. Rebecca had been trying to rebuild her relationship with Rosalind after everything they had been through. It seemed that the viscountess apologised every time they were in each other's company, less bothered about what the ton thought of her and her family's reputation after everything that had happened.

'Can you not remove your eyes from your wife for a single moment Fane?' Benjamin gibed as he and Sir Thomas joined Alexander, handing him a large drink.

'I remember being the same on my wedding day. It is nothing to be ashamed of, dear boy', Thomas smiled, while affectionately looking at his own wife.

'It will happen to you soon enough, Ben. A lady will breeze into your life and steal your heart.'

Alexander was aware of a snort at his back as he conversed with the two gentlemen. Emma stood nearby, holding a glass of champagne, her eyes slightly glazed over after having enjoyed one too many glasses.

'I pity the poor lady that catches your roving eye, my Lord,' she scoffed.

'Emma, I do believe you have had too much champagne', Alexander replied, trying not to snigger at her comment that was directed at the young viscount.

'You will be delighted that it will not be you then, my Lady. Or is that jealousy I detect?' Ben countered, raising his glass as if toasting her.

Standing with her mouth partly open in outrage, Emma responded to his comment, 'Ohhhh, I *hate* you Turner, you conceited fool,' before hastily taking her leave. Turner laughed at the theatrics while Alexander and Sir Thomas observed the interplay between the two.

It was soon time for everyone to leave, allowing the newlyweds to begin their married life together. The last guest had barely left when Alexander threw his new wife over his shoulder and ran up the stairs as she squealed in delight. When they reached his chambers, he playfully smacked her backside demanding she remove her dress.

'I do not take orders from you, your Grace, just because I am now your wife,' she chuckled with her arms crossed over her chest.

'As you wish', he replied, disregarding her response while unbuttoning his jacket.

It did not take long before he stood fully naked in front of her while she remained dressed in her bridal gown. Rebecca admired her husband's athletic physique as he turned to walk away, admiring his strong back, firm buttocks and muscular thighs. As he strode towards the adjoining room, she knew he was up to something by the way he had smirked at her while undressing.

The sight of his nakedness had made her even more desperate for his touch, but she was not going to give in to his demands so quickly. They still enjoyed tormenting each other and playing games; delaying the inevitable always made their passionate encounters even more pleasurable. Alexander had now disappeared fully naked into Rebecca's chambers, hoping that she would follow him. He had asked the servants to prepare a large bath with drops of lavender oil for their wedding night, remembering her flirtatious comment from all those weeks ago. Eagerly climbing into the warm water, he lay back anticipating the arrival of his new bride.

Rebecca could smell the lavender emanating from the adjoining room once her husband had opened the doors. She had wanted to delay a little longer but could not wait another minute if what she suspected was true, removing her shoes, stockings, and the pins from her hair, but keeping on her wedding dress. Desiring that her new husband remove it for her, she dashed through the doors, halting at the glorious sight of the duke lying lazily in the warm bath, hands clasped behind his head, appraising her lustfully when she had glided into the room. A bottle of champagne and two glasses rested on the floor next to the large bathtub.

'You wished to experience one of my lavender baths, if I recall, wife', he growled as he sat up revealing his strong chest, the dark hair glistening with droplets of water.

Rebecca went to her husband, leaning over the bath and inhaling the scent that would always remind her of him. She slipped her hand beneath the water, licking her lips as she wrapped her hand around his hardening shaft.

'Oh God, keep doing that, my darling,' he gasped pulling her down for a kiss.

They kissed until it became more frenzied. As Rebecca continued to stroke him faster, without warning she felt herself being pulled into the bath, the water spilling over the sides onto the rug.

'My beautiful dress, it will be ruined,' she yelped as she became immersed in the water.

'To hell with the dress! I will buy you one hundred dresses,' he rasped, kissing her neck.

He had quickly learned that Rebecca enjoyed it when he cursed or behaved like a rogue when they were in the throes of passion. Pulling her to sit on top of him, it was not long before he was inside her, water splashing as they frantically made love for the first time as husband and wife.

The sight of her riding him in the water while still wearing her soaking wet wedding gown was the most erotic thing Alexander had ever seen. Deciding that the dress was ruined anyway he ripped the front, before lifting her breasts over her undergarments so he could suck on her rosy, pink nipple. Rebecca panted his name louder as she reached her pinnacle feeling the warm sensation inside her when her husband roared in pleasure as he filled her with his seed.

Lying in bed, satiated after spending the day drinking champagne and making love, the newlyweds reminisced about when they first met, admitting that they were instantly attracted to each other but never thought they would fall in love as they had. Face-to-face, each of them fighting sleep, too tired to speak, Rebecca gave her new husband a chaste kiss on the cheek before they both drifted into a peaceful slumber.

EPILOGUE

The book they had been discussing balanced precariously on her swollen belly, the Duchess of Sandison complained to her friends, 'I am so fat that I cannot even see my feet!'

'You look utterly radiant, Rebecca, darling,' Katherine insisted. 'You and his Grace will have the most beautiful babies.'

'*Babies?* Oh no, no, no, Katherine that will *not* do at all. I am not going through this again,' she grumbled while trying to get herself comfortable due to her back aching more than normal.

Rebecca was due to give birth any day and her friends had come round to discuss a new novel to take her mind off things. But all she could do was wriggle in her seat unable to get herself comfortable. Although she had been ecstatic, as was her husband when it was confirmed that she was with child, the last few weeks had not been the best. She complained to the duke about swollen ankles and back pain, while he rubbed her feet and dried her tears when she could not button up her larger dresses.

While Rebecca complained, Alexander could not help lusting after his new duchess. She had never looked so desirable as far as he was concerned. The vision of her plump breasts and rounded belly made it difficult for him to think of anything other than bending her over his desk as he took her from behind, while his hands caressed her huge breasts.

'I cannot wait to meet my niece or nephew; I am already excited to read them some of our favourite stories,' Emma gushed.

As the ladies laughed at the idea of reading gothic novels to a small child, they saw Rebecca flinch, leaning forward before yelling out. 'Oh, *ow* ... Oh no, I think the babe might be coming,' she screeched as she felt another sharp pain. 'I do not think I can do this!'

'Of course, you can do it, Rebecca. You will be holding a tiny babe in your arms before you know it,' Emma said before she quickly hurried out of the room, shouting for her brother who was currently working in his study, refusing to leave the house with his wife being so close to giving birth. The door immediately flew open, and Alexander rushed out.

'Is it time? Where is Rebecca?' he panicked, unaware that his sister was trying not to laugh at his excitable behaviour.

Further down the hall, the weeping duchess was being helped to her rooms.

'Let us get you to your chambers, your Grace', a young maid fussed, while another was summoned to call for the physician and mid wife.

Alexander's footsteps could be heard throughout the house as he ran down the hallway to be with his wife, arriving just as she reached her room, cursing in a very unladylike fashion.

'My darling are you well?' he worried as he reached out to her.

'Of course, I am *not* well … I am in agony, and it is all *your* fault, Fane', she shouted in between sobs.

'I am so sorry. If I could change places with you right now, I promise you I would,' Alexander soothed.

'I doubt that very much, your Grace. Just get out of my sight,' she screamed, while bent over clutching her belly.

Although upset at his wife's words, he knew she did not mean it as they loved each other dearly, not having spent a single night apart since they were married. He was already thinking how he could tease her later.

The young duchess's friends stood open-mouthed but said nothing as they hovered a little distance behind, trying to disguise their giggling upon hearing Rebecca's outburst. They knew she loved the duke more than life itself and they were sure they would all laugh about it when she had the new babe in her arms and her husband at her side.

Alexander had never felt so helpless in his life. Unable to sit still, he nervously paced back and forth outside Rebecca's chamber, desperate to be the one who was holding her hand. He did not care that it was not the done thing for the babe's father to be at the mother's side. If she had called for him, he would have gone in without a second thought, and to hell with propriety.

The sound of his wife's screams and the odd curse coming from her bedchamber was not something you would expect to hear from a young lady of her breeding, but Alexander loved that about her. She had not conformed to society's rules when she became his wife; she mainly continued her life as she had before, loved and respected by all the servants and acquaintances alike. What he did not love were the sounds of his beloved in pain and being powerless to do anything to ease it. Noticing the look of anguish on his face, Emma placed her hand gently on her brother's arm.

'It will be fine Alexander, she is strong. Rose will not let anything happen to her,' she soothed. Now that Rebecca and Rose had discovered a strong sisterly bond, she was the one chosen to hold her hand throughout.

'I do not think I could carry on if anything happened to her, Emma. I never thought that I could love another as much as I do my wife.' Alexander stood with his palms flat against the wall, so his back was facing his sister.

'Do not speak in such a way, Alex. She has the best doctor in the city tending her. You just need to be patient. It will all be over soon.'

Rebecca had fallen pregnant quicker than they had anticipated, although it should have been of little surprise due to them being unable to keep their hands off of each other. There had been more than one embarrassing situation when a servant had walked in on them making love in his study or catching sight of the duke with his head between his wife's thighs.

Dr Fleming had assured the couple they could continue marital relations without any harm to mother or child, so they keenly accepted his professional advice and did just that. It was only the day previous that Rebecca had interrupted Alexander at work and demanded he lift her skirts before making love to her bent over the chaise. She had screamed his name as he gladly obliged; the screams that he now heard from behind the closed doors were unlike the ones he had become accustomed to when he pleasured her, and he could not bear it for much longer.

~

It was dawn when Rose opened the door, the faint cry of a newborn could be heard from further in the room. Rose's eyes were red-rimmed and tired, a slight sheen of perspiration settled on her brow as she gave Alexander the biggest smile, her arms signalling for him to come closer.

'She is well and asks for you, your Grace', Rose sniffed with tears in her eyes. She had barely finished speaking before Alexander was in the room at his wife's bedside.

Rebecca had fallen instantly in love with her new child, unable to look away from the wide-eyed babe, which was why she failed to notice her husband when he had cautiously entered the room.

'Rebecca', he whispered, reaching out to stroke her damp hair, motioning for everyone in the room to leave so they could have some time alone.

'Alex, we have a son, a beautiful baby boy', she beamed while cradling the infant in her arms. He kissed her tenderly on the lips before his eyes dropped to look at the little bundle.

'Do you wish to hold him, my darling?' she asked tenderly.

All Alexander could do was nod and open his arms. The duke and duchess said very little to each other. All they could do was look at their newborn in awe, Alexander cradling his new son while his wife drifted in and out of sleep. His eyes glistened as he watched the two most important people in his life., hardly able to believe they were his and how he had gotten so lucky.

The sound of a gentle tap on the door was followed by his beaming sister peering into the room before she tip-toed in, rousing the duke from his current thoughts. She was followed by Felicity, Matilda, and Katherine, all trying to be as quiet as they could. Alexander looked up and smiled, having grown quite fond of his wife's friends and the special bond they shared.

'A boy, Emma. I have a son,' he said softly, not wanting to wake his wife.

~

The Duke and Duchess of Sandison had waited a few months before holding a ball in honour of their newborn son and heir. The invitations were the most sought after in the ton, but the young couple also wanted to invite the special people in their lives, such as Flora and her new husband George, who were also godparents to their son, who they had named James. They also invited the doctor who delivered their son, who was also the baby's namesake.

The duke and duchess stood to the side of the floor as they watched the festivities, the orchestra in full flow while couples in the first throes of romance danced and flirted in time to the music.

'Have I ever told you how handsome you are, husband?' Rebecca said while admiring the duke in his evening wear.

Smiling rakishly, Alexander leaned over so he could whisper in his wife's ear, 'Have I ever told you how much I love you wife or would you rather I show you,' he growled, discreetly nibbling on her lobe. Today had been the first time since the birth of James that they had properly made love, and he knew she would be desperate for him again when they returned home this evening.

'You know me so well, your Grace', she purred, leaning into his touch.

'Can you refrain from such behaviour in public, your Graces?' The voice from behind complained, albeit with a humorous tone.

'Jealous are you, my Lord?' Rebecca teased as Benjamin shook his head in fake disgust.

'Not jealous. Just slightly nauseous', he laughed while pushing his wayward hair away from his forehead.

'Your hair still needs cutting, Turner', Alexander remarked as his wife nodded her head in agreement.

'I have told you before, the ladies love it,' the handsome viscount bragged.

'Ladies?' Alexander queried. 'I thought your rakish days were over and you were looking for a wife?'

'Yes, that is the plan, but I have yet to find anyone suitable,' Benjamin moaned. 'All the ladies I have been introduced to are so dull and insipid.'

'Maybe you are trying too hard, Ben. I found mine when I was not looking,' the duke boasted.

'Yes, well that is highly unusual, but I do envy you. Rebecca is an exceptional young woman,' Ben said with a congratulatory slap on his friend's shoulder.

'She also has several unmarried exceptional friends, or had you not noticed,' Alexander asked.

'Do you include your own sister in that?' Ben joked.

'Ha. I do not know who would kill who first. My sister has quite the temper where you are concerned,' the Duke replied, raising an eyebrow.

Viscount Turner had been on the receiving end of that temper more than once but took huge delight in it every time. Especially when her eyes grew larger, and her cheeks were flushed in the most attractive shade of pink.

~

Rebecca had left her husband's side and was now huddled in the corner with her friends, like old times.

'Married life treats you well,' Lady Matilda gushed, 'As does motherhood. You look wonderful Rebecca.'

'It does, very much so. I cannot wait for each of you to fall in love. I wonder which one of you will be next.' Rebecca eyed all of her friends, waiting for a response. 'Emma. My husband is keen for you to make a match this season, as is your mother. Has anyone garnered your attention?' she pried, a glint in her eye.

'Perhaps she will marry Viscount Turner, as he is such good friends with his grace?' Felicity joked, knowing how much Emma disliked the man. 'And so very handsome,' she winked.

'If you think him so handsome, why do you not marry him, as I would rather cut off my own leg?' she uttered while shaking her head in repulsion.

The ladies giggled with Emma at the very thought of her removing her limb rather than marry the dashing viscount, when the very man they spoke of appeared, as if by magic.

Dipping his head, Benjamin apologised for interrupting their conversation before unashamedly looking down at Lady Emma's leg, so she knew that he had overheard her comment, before returning his attention to his hostess.

'Your Grace. Sadly, I must take my leave due to an urgent matter that must be attended to. I would like to thank you for a wonderful evening,' he apologised to Rebecca then bowed respectfully to the other ladies, his eyes lingering on Emma for slightly longer, cheekily raising an eyebrow when she returned the gaze. She could not look away from him quick enough for fear of blushing.

Emma felt quite cross as she watched the viscount walk away. He had deliberately stared at her, knowing it would cause her some embarrassment. She continued to watch as he headed towards the exit, nodding at various ladies when he passed, occasionally running his fingers through his irritatingly beautiful hair. This had not gone unnoticed by the younger ladies of the ton, who began fanning themselves enthusiastically when he passed. She hated how she thought his hair beautiful: it was the thing that she had fancied most about him when she had been a foolish young girl.

'Do you think he is meeting a lady?' Felicity enquired with a smirk, wiggling her perfect brows. 'He does have a somewhat dubious reputation.'

'I do hope not. He has been telling Alexander that those days are over as he looks for his viscountess,' Rebecca revealed.

'This might be an interesting season, after all,' Emma declared.

'How so?' her friends said in unison.

'Watching the viscount change his ways and choose his bride will be very interesting indeed. I do not believe for a minute he will last the season without taking a lover', Emma stated as she glanced around the ballroom at the various young ladies trying to snare themselves a husband. 'I think it could be quite amusing, that is all'.

'I disagree, Emma. He was very convincing. I think he secretly wants to fall in love but does not want to admit it,' Rebecca said. 'I have grown extremely fond of the viscount; he has always been very kind to me.'

Emma could not think of a response before her brother, the Duke of Sandison, had joined them. 'What are you ladies gossiping about?' he enquired, placing a chaste kiss on his wife's cheek.

'Nothing that will be of interest to you, my darling', Rebecca answered before covering her mouth to yawn.

'Are you very tired, my love?', Alexander asked his wife.

'I am getting quite tired now, Alex. It has been a long day. Do you think I could retire without any of the guests noticing?' Rebecca asked her husband with a sly look.

Alexander suspected that she wasn't as tired as she professed, judging by the way her eyes lustfully travelled over his person. Rebecca yawned several more times before bidding her friends goodnight, who were also unconvinced that she was as tired as she made out.

~

In the bedchamber they had shared every night since they were married, Rebecca wore nothing but a pair of red silk stockings that had been purchased especially for her husband's pleasure, desperate for the duke to join her. She had whispered how much she needed him as she left the ball a short time earlier, his desire obvious by the way he gazed at her when she walked away.

Rebecca had heard her husband's footsteps approaching, giving her time to seductively position herself on an armchair. Crossing and uncrossing her stocking-clad legs several times, deciding on what the most seductive position would be, she lounged back into the cushions ready for her husband.

The door eventually swung open and when the duke saw his duchess sitting naked in front of him, he kicked the door closed with so much force that it might have been heard as far away as the stables.

'Good evening, your Grace', she purred.

Alexander could not take his eyes off his wife as he stripped, leaving a trail of clothing behind him. Rebecca chewed on her bottom lip as she admired his naked form, instantly making him go hard.

'Good evening, Duchess,' he answered, taking her hands as he pulled her from the chair, kissing her passionately.

Lifting her so she could wrap her legs around his waist, his hands stroked the silk that adorned her perfectly shaped calves before they both fell onto the firm mattress. It was not long before Rebecca was straddling her husband, riding him until they were both completely satisfied and lying wrapped in each other's arms.

'I love you, Alexander Fane', she said sheepishly while stroking his back, 'And I am sorry I was so horrid to you for those months that I was with child. I said some truly awful things.'

'Mmmm.you did indeed my love, I believe you might have a lot of making up to do if you want my full forgiveness,' he smirked roguishly, before lightly smacking her on the bottom.

The End

Printed in Great Britain
by Amazon